HERO OF HEARTBREAK HILL

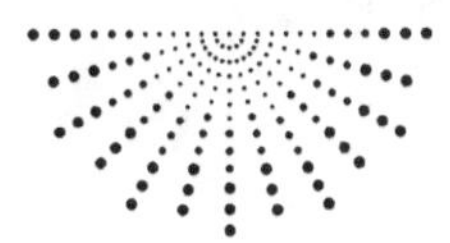

IMOGENE NIX

DEDICATION

Please note - this book is written in Australian English hence the spelling of certain words.

Having lived in a range of small rural and regional townships during my adult life, I had lots of experience to draw upon when writing Hero of Heartbreak Hill.
I have loosely based Heartbreak Hill on one township in particular (not naming the actual location of course!) It was a small yet welcoming community—like those you read about in so many rural romances and yet, this one really existed (and still does!)
I need to thank my husband for his background knowledge of Local Government. His input allowed me free rein to allow Connor to be both believable and interesting. As for Kelly, well I was able to draw upon my many years as a teacher. I suppose you could say this book is the culmination of 23 years worth of experience!
Thank you to Joanne and Erin for coming up with this idea and giving me the chance to participate in the Kiss Me boxed set where this was originally published.
Many thanks to Jan and Kate for critiquing and to Tracey, who is

the worlds best Beta reader. To the wonderful Sassie for once more editing my work.

To my family and friends - those who know of the story and encouraged me while I wrote it.

To google for images of sexy bare chested men, pictures of my hero and of course heroine. Without those this book wouldn't be half hot as he is!

And, as always, dear reader... Thank you for choosing to read this story.

Imogene

CHAPTER ONE

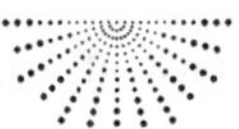

Connor wasn't sure if it was the day, the heat or the township itself that caused the first twinges of unease. He sat, looking at the small squat window of his office, the slats of the metal blinds obscuring his sight. The land stretched for miles in an uninterrupted vista of red and rocks. Here and there it was interspersed with ant mounds, but the moonscape, as he'd come to describe it, looked never ending.

Heartbreak Hill—he'd been here five and a half months. Long enough to know that the landscape stretched for a hundred kilometres before colliding with the border of South Australia and New South Wales.

He sighed, the aging air conditioner in his office chugged under the battering heat. Forty degrees outside and it had to be at least thirty in his office.

Staring at the screen before him, Connor considered the budget of his small council. Heartbreak Hill had a long, though not terribly illustrious, history—one he'd become part of after relocating from a larger township.

The tap at the door pulled Connor from his introspection. Penny, the executive officer shared between himself and the mayor and the CEO, stuck her head around the corner.

"Frank and Jim were hoping you'd have a few minutes. They have something important they need to discuss with you."

He started to rise but she shook her head. "They'll join you." Then in a flash the little red-haired woman was gone. He wondered why they'd want to see him in his office. If they'd requested him in either the Mayor or CEO's office, well, that would have meant something ominous.

Jim and Frank—Francis Servier the Second, the Mayor always joked—entered the room and Jim slid the door closed with a click, then settled into the seats opposite him. He couldn't quite contain the concern that jittered through him. "So, Jim, Frank? What's up?"

Jim smiled. "Nervous are you?"

His gaze narrowed on the older man. "Maybe a bit."

Frank laughed. "Well, that's not exactly a surprise. You've been in cutthroat councils up until now. We work differently here, you should have figured that out. You've been with us, what, four months?"

"Five and a half. My probation ended two General Meetings back."

Inhaling deeply didn't help as the butterflies became dragons, the heat in his belly making him clench but Connor refused to betray his roiling emotions in front of these men. He might respect them—like them even—but he refused to show his uncertainty. That was a lesson he'd learned well in the coastal councils.

Jim frowned, sighed and settled deeper in his seat. "Frank and I have been talking. I got my latest results and they weren't good." He scratched his head. "I need chemo and Lisa and I both agree, it's time to head home. Spend time with the kids. Retire."

The words were a blow, but he could appreciate Lisa's request. They'd been here for nearly seven years while their children had married, graduated college and started their own lives.

"I'm sorry to hear that Jim. Working for you has given me the opportunity to learn a lot."

Frank shot forward in his chair. "It has, and it's given us time to take a good look at you. The councillors and I agree: We'd like you to step up into the role. You know the running of the place already. The workers respect you and you're not in it for the glory. Plus you're young and eager. We need someone in the top job we can count on. Who won't go running off at the drop of a hat. The job is yours if you want it."

Shock rippled. Him? Step into Jim's job?

"I... Uh, I need time to consider." He hadn't thought this would happen yet. There'd been talk over the last month of him perhaps taking on the acting role while Jim sought cancer treatment, but this hadn't ever been raised.

"Good." Frank nodded. "We're not looking for someone who makes flippant choices and decisions. When you're ready, come find me and we can discuss packages."

Connor's mouth didn't work, so he sat there, numb in his seat.

"I expect that will be tomorrow or the day after, right?" On that, Frank and Jim left the room while he stared at the door.

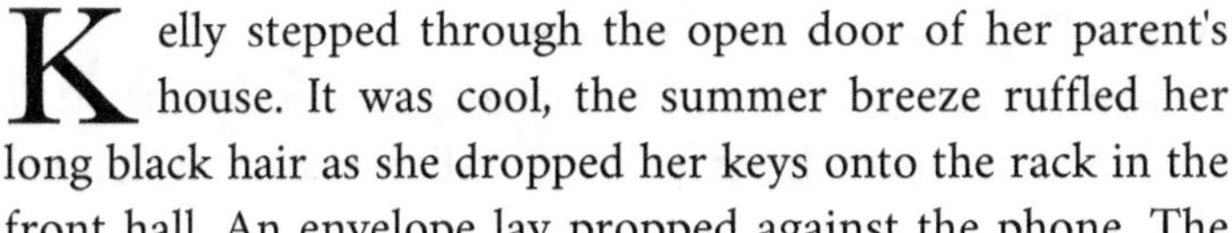

Kelly stepped through the open door of her parent's house. It was cool, the summer breeze ruffled her long black hair as she dropped her keys onto the rack in the front hall. An envelope lay propped against the phone. The thick white paper embossed with the name of her solicitors caught her attention and for a moment she forgot to breathe.

"Kelly, is that you?"

The sound of her mother's voice floated through the air.

"Yeah."

"Good. A letter came for you today. It looks important."

Her hand shook as she reached for it. The weight of it was slight and yet the importance of what it contained would change her life. Give her back the freedom she needed to begin living again.

David—her soon to be ex-husband—had stripped so much from her. Not just her freedom, but her sense of safety and self.

They'd only been married nine months when she'd broken away and run. She'd moved into a tiny rental, thinking she'd be safe. Kelly'd been shattered when he'd tracked her down after her first solicitor's receptionist had accidentally shipped her paperwork to David.

Memories of the crashing door, splintered wood flying and the screaming had left her with nightmares for ages after. Kelly bit her lip unable to banish the memories of her flight.

She'd filed for divorce as soon as she could; the date circled in red on her calendar seven months in advance.

With shaking fingers she slid the flap up. Her entire life encapsulated in the heading, Decree Absolute. Silent tears welled, burning her cheeks in a flood, even as the sound of footsteps echoed on the tiled floor.

"Kelly? Is it what you—" She nodded in the direction of her mother—Sarah. "Are you alright?" Enfolding her arms around Kelly, her mother tugged her close.

"I'm good." She hiccupped, realising her mother couldn't really understand the depths of relief this missive had given her.

"Come through to the kitchen, I'll make you a cup of tea and we can decide on dinner. Something special, I think."

Speaking through the bubble of emotion proved difficult. "No. I, um. I think I'll go have a bath, mum. A long soak because I need to think some stuff over. The only thing I do know is, now that I have this, I want to look for a job away from here."

The look on Sarah's face told Kelly she'd surprised and hurt her. It took a moment to realise she needed to explain in more detail. "Not that I want to go away, but I need to re-start my life, mum. I need to be Kelly Chester. Not David Windover's ex, or the girl who married the psycho. I can't be a victim and this is the first step to reclaiming the real me."

"But, you could do that here." The strain in her mother's voice tore at Kelly, but she had to be strong.

"I could. But here they know me. I mean, most of them remember the reason I was off work for a month. They remember David's attack and I need to break free of the memories and the careful way they talk around me. I can't do that here."

"Well, if you're sure, Kel. Just, don't be away too long."

The sigh Kelly released was long and full of understanding. Her parents had supported her through everything. She'd married David after knowing him six months. The whirlwind romance had concerned them but she'd reassured them it was right.

When she'd left David, they'd helped her pack up while he was away on a business trip. The attack in the mall, where he'd caught sight of her had ended up with two passers-by pulling him off, and left her with a brutal slice to her shoulder. Her parents had been there through all of that. They'd understood her need to go to the shelter and be with those who understood. They'd attended the hearing after he'd been arrested. Heard him screaming out from the dock that she should get her backside back to him.

They'd weathered the nightmares that had gradually melted away since moving in with them.

"It's something I need to do, mum. Please. I need you to understand that?"

"We will. We will support you, whatever decision you make." On a sigh her mother pulled away. "Go have your soak, but I'm ordering pizza for half past six. That gives you an hour and a half."

Kelly smiled and kissed her mother on the cheek. "I'll be out by then."

~

Connor entered his house. The oppressive heat beating down on him. It might be thirty degrees now that the sun dropped below the horizon, but he was damned pleased he'd turned on the air conditioner this morning.

His mind still whirred with the things Jim and Frank had said. Could he fill the role? Was another four years here achievable? He thought of his mother, Niamh. He needed to talk with her and gain her counsel. Checking his watch, he realised she'd be home in an hour from her pottery class.

They'd been close for as long as he could remember. Niamh never marrying, always claiming he was her priority.

She and Bao Xi Wan had planned to marry when they'd discovered her pregnancy, but he'd been killed in car accident just weeks before their wedding and three months prior to Niamh giving birth. She'd had been forced to raise her half Chinese half Scottish son by herself.

It hadn't been easy. He glanced at a photo of her on the wall. She'd finally met an older man and they'd hit it off.

Connor expected great things from Simon, but for now, he still sought his mother as his first point of call.

Indecision weighed him down and he grunted, checked the clock again. Six twenty-seven. Maybe he should go pump some weights to release the pressure building up in his system. Usually that would settle him, yet tonight he wondered if it would work.

He moved to the kitchen pouring a glass of water from the carafe in the fridge and looked out his window.

The tiny town of five hundred and forty-two was close-knit. Those who'd grown up here left to meet their partners and the few who returned brought spouses and children. It was great if you were married.

Connor scraped his blunt fingers through his dark hair. They didn't get a lot of single women out here and he wanted a family, and at twenty-eight it seemed past time to settle down.

"At the end of this contract, I'll be thirty-two and no woman. I'm not sure that's good odds."

His best friend, Martin had laughed when he'd moved west. "You're going to die an old single man, while I'll still be rolling in chicks." Each time he logged onto Facebook it showed Martin with a new girl on his arm.

He reached for the phone, then shook his head. "Martin will be busy and I know what he'll say."

He shrugged and tugged at his shirt, a shower was the first step in winding down for the night and besides, the mail delivery today included the local school flyer. With that thought he padded down the hall.

~

Kelly sat at the computer, her fingers hovering over the keyboard. "Go on, Kelly. Do it." Whispering to herself had become an integral part of facing life head on. She couldn't escape the truths when she spoke them aloud and over time, she'd taken to weighing up options verbally too.

Her fingers touched the keys and the machine roared to life. She connected the Wi-Fi and brought up the browser, entering the address she'd memorised. The screen filled with the search choices of the education website and she tapped in vacancies. The screen filled again and she bit her lip.

She'd been drawn to a western posting before, yet when she'd met and married David, she'd discounted it. The yearning hadn't ever passed though, and Kelly tapped in South West Queensland.

The selections were more sparse. Scrolling through the options took time. On the last page, though, Kelly spied one that interested her.

Regional/Rural. Early Education. Contract Placement.

Depressing a button opened a file detailing the location, the schools information and other aspects of the placement.

It took a moment to print the three pages of particulars and Kelly looked up the school using a search engine. Forty-three pupils. Two separate classes. Junior consisting of Prep to grade three and Senior was grades four to six. A series of photos of the school intrigued Kelly. Next she scoured the net searching for information about the township and opportunities in Heartbreak Hill.

It felt right and when her mother called, "Kel, dinner's here!" she'd made the decision to apply for the position.

With a smile on her face, Kelly turned off the computer, grabbed up the papers and headed for the kitchen.

A new phase in her life could be opening right now. It had never felt so good.

CHAPTER TWO

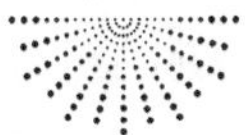

The sun was dipping over the horizon as Kelly drove over the old wooden bridge at the approach to Heartbreak Hill. The nine-hour drive had been far harder to achieve than she'd planned, and it was with a fair degree of thankfulness that she remembered the booking her mother had insisted on at the local motel. The truck with her furniture was due to arrive tomorrow and she'd move into the tiny teachers accommodation immediately.

On the left, the school stood at the very entrance of town: an old fashioned wood building of two stories, sat in a patch of green. The further she drove though, the more it became obvious that was about the only patch of green in the township.

The rolling landscape of scrubby trees had ended about thirty minutes before the bridge over a dry creek bed. The shrubs and trees that bordered the creek appeared stunted and stressed.

The kangaroos hopping about were lean and the heat of summer stole her breath. She wound the window back up. Air conditioning would be her friend.

The township was as compact as Kelly had been led to understand, with houses dotted here and there. One small shop, a post office and a pub filled the commercial zone. On her left the library, a wooden lean-to affair and a newer office for the municipal council were bordered by an old fashioned service station boasting three bowsers, a car dealership and at the end, the one and only motel in town.

"I hope I can do this." Her stomach clenched hard as she pulled into the gravelled parking lot and turned off the car.

Above her, a light flickered on, and a large swarm of bugs appeared. Kelly grabbed her keys, bag and phone and stepped out of the vehicle. The office lay straight ahead and Kelly locked her car and made her way toward it. Music filtered from inside. A country and western tune filling the air and she had to work hard to stop herself from screwing up her nose. She much preferred the dulcet tones of her favourite singer, but she'd moved west to experience a new way of life.

Pushing the door open, she noted the jangle of the bells that hung on the side.

A head popped through the curtain of hanging vinyl strips. "Hi? Are you after a room? We're kind of booked up."

"I'm Kelly Chester? I have a booking for a room for three nights."

The woman pulled out the ledger and peered down. "Oh, Chester. Three nights. Yep, we've got you. You're the new teacher aren't you?"

Kelly nodded. "Yes, I've just arrived."

"Good. I've got a trucker waiting to see if you're turning up otherwise he'll have to see if he can get a room at the caravan park and that's not exactly a popular choice, you know?" The woman nattered away as if Kelly had any idea what she was talking about.

"Now, here's your key. You're in room two. It has air-conditioning but the fridge isn't working so well. The pub across the road is only cooking for, " she looked down, "another ten minutes, so if you're planning on dinner, you'd better head now."

With that the woman who'd introduced herself as Penny, pushed her out the door and pointed. "Old Kev, who runs it is a stickler. Don't hang around or you'll miss out."

The door shut and for a moment Kelly just stood there, stunned at the way she'd been ushered out, then shrugged. If she didn't order now there'd be no hope. She stashed the room key in her bag and strode up the road.

Entering the pub was like stepping into a totally new planet. Small groups of people clustered here and there, a few held up the bar and she felt lost. On a deep breath, Kelly headed over and waved down the publican. "I'd like to order a meal. What do you have?"

"Tonight is roast or fish. Battered or crumbed barra. And pork. Take your pick."

She blinked and made a split second decision. "The fish. Does it come with—"

"Chips and salad. Wanna drink?"

The terse question threw her off. "Umm could I get a chardonnay please?"

"Fifteen-seventy."

Old Kev might look seventy and a bit but it was clear his mind was a steel trap. Kelly fished around in her bag and withdrew her purse.

"We don't do card. Cash only."

Glancing down, Kelly was pleased to see a twenty-dollar note in her purse and handed it over.

"Find a seat and I'll bring it over."

Only one table remained, right next to the biggest group, around ten people all wearing a uniform emblazoned with the council name and logo.

Self-conscious though she was, Kelly wandered over and

sat down, pulling out her phone. As she'd left, Kelly had promised to text her mother when she'd arrived so proceeded to do so.

The drink was delivered by a young girl just as Kelly popped her phone back in her bag. "Thanks."

The girl smiled and started to back away as the most good looking man Kelly had ever seen headed in their direction.

"Hey Connor. Congratulations! It must be nice, now that it's official."

The man, he had to be in his late twenties grinned and Kelly couldn't control her involuntary reaction. The shiver of excitement catching her by surprise.

"Thanks Nina. Yeah, now I just hope I can live up to it."

His dark eyes shone in the fluorescent lighting overhead, reminding her of warm gooey chocolate. His hair appeared to be the darkest of silks, close cut so every inch of his face was clearly defined, from the high brow to the wickedly slashing cheek and jawline.

Her gaze travelled south, noting the well-defined lips, muscular shoulders and the fit of his white shirt and black dress pants meant she needed to stop herself before she began licking her lips.

When he grinned, the little bit of sense she scrabbled onto fled and her mouth sagged open.

He winked at her and passed on by and the heat of a vicious blush flared.

"Don't worry. We all reacted like that the first time he turned up here. You've only got a problem though if you're planning on staying in town."

The girl—Nina's—words broke the spell and Kelly turned to look at her. "Oh. I'm here as the new teacher."

The girl grinned. "Oh that's awesome. You'll be swamped." With those words she retreated back behind the bar.

Connor handed over the present to Jim, the farewell gift from the staff was wrapped in letterhead and tied with a ribbon the exact colour of the logo. "Jim, I know I haven't been here the longest, but I've learned so much from you. I hope I can do half as good a job as I know you would, going forward."

The attending staff clapped their hands as Jim grimaced. He nodded to Connor and stood, shuffling from side to side, hands jammed deep into his pockets.

"I wasn't planning on leaving yet, but the truth is I have cancer. Some of you worked it out but only Frank and Connor knew the truth. We're moving home so I'm closer to the treatment centre and family. The prognosis isn't as good as we'd like but it's better, according to the oncologist, if I'm not always travelling back and forth for treatment. The councillors and mayor have offered me time off but I think in all fairness this is the best outcome for all.

"I need to thank you all for your kind, good wishes and assistance over the years. I'm sure Connor will steer the council on a strong path."

He glanced over Jim's shoulder to see the woman, attractive dark haired with pale skin rose. When Nina had served him his one beer she'd whispered, "she's the new teacher."

Was is a conspiracy? Maybe. An attempt at matchmaking? He wasn't totally sure having never been on the receiving end of such assistance, but it seemed like that was the deal.

Even as she left the pub, the subtle sway of her hips mesmerised him and he realised that her hair was exceptionally long. The strands that had escaped her messy bun swayed against her lower back drawing his gaze down to her tight backside and long shapely legs.

He swallowed and dragged his attention back to those around him with difficulty as the door swung shut.

Interest, the kind he'd never before experienced slammed him hard in the gut. I'll have to make time to meet her properly and talk to her, he told himself before immersed himself once more in the subdued atmosphere of Jim's get together.

~

K elly slumped against the counter. The shabbiness of the house was both a surprise and a disappointment. The colour scheme of 70's khaki and ochre married with the avocado green on the laminate worktop.

Not for the first time today, she was pleased to have moved two weeks before school resumed. It would give her time to organise her home as well as prepare for the new school year.

The removalists, at least, had set up the furniture, so she didn't have to lug anything around, or find screws and hex keys. In fact her main concern was to search out the box she'd labelled linen and the one tagged 'Open First'. At least then she could make a cup of coffee, cook a basic meal and take a shower. Gazing around at the piles of boxes though, her heart sank once more. Lunchtime loomed, and she'd need to head to the shop in a few minutes to gather the items on her grocery list. Kelly just hoped they carried all the things she was used to.

Slipping on her shoes, she grabbed up her purse and keys. If she went now, she could settle in, find the cords for the television then set up her router and internet connections and fill the fridge happily humming away in the background.

The heat of the sun beat down and the red landscape once more filled her with trepidation. Had she bitten off more than she could chew? She chewed her lip and trudged to the car. Getting in was like entering a furnace. The seats were scorching even as she tugged on the shade cover and with the air blowing it took several minutes for the car to cool sufficiently that she could close the car door.

Reversing, she silently ran through her shopping list in her mind. Washing powder, dishwashing liquid, milk, eggs, flour... The blare of a car horn shattered her concentration and she slammed her foot on the brake. The car lurched and stalled as she turned beet red, heat radiating from the skin of her face.

Drat! The cute guy from the pub! She wished she could crawl into a hole but that wasn't an option.

The slam of a car door echoed and she groaned. "Oh, man."

He must have made his way over because the rapping on the car window had her tugging at the winder. "Um, look I'm really sorry. I didn't see you—"

"You were so lost in yourself that you nearly took the fence out." She peered out the window. He was right of course, the rear of the car was no longer on the driveway and was mere inches from the metal mesh fence.

"I was going over my shopping list."

He grinned at her. "I can't say that's ever left me out of it before, but if that floats your boat and all..." He reached out. "I'm Connor, welcome to Heartbreak Hill."

Glancing down to his hand then up to his face, the heat flared again. "I... Hi, I'm Kelly. I'm the new teacher."

"I know." His grin widened and she wanted to sink into the floor of her car. "Oh."

"Nina told me. It's like that around here."

"Ah. And you come off a station?" Her natural inquisitiveness raised its head. The need to know more about this gorgeous man hummed in her veins.

"No. I work for the council."

"Oh." Though dying to know more, Kelly stopped herself before asking. He intrigued her but she wasn't looking for a man. No matter that he looked like sin on legs, she'd be strong. After all, the last time she'd made a snap decision it had taken years to extricate herself from the mess.

"Well, thank you for saving the fence. I'll keep a better eye out next time." He'd take the hint, take himself and his exotic body and genuine niceness and leave her alone, she hoped.

"Throwing me out?" He hooked his thumbs into the belt he wore and grinned.

"Oh, no. But I don't have coffee or milk and the house is a mess, otherwise I might invite you in for a drink." Kelly couldn't stop the sassy bite in her voice, then almost cringed. Clearly she hadn't learned well enough from the David debacle.

"That's okay. I was popping by to let you know we have a community barbeque tonight and since you won't have seen the flyer yet at the post office, I was inviting you to come along."

His smile grew wider and his eyes twinkled. The cold centre in her stomach wobbled and began to melt just a little.

"Oh... Um, that's very nice of you."

"Five thirty behind the Council office. There's a gazebo there. If you can't find a fold out chair, don't stress. I'll make sure there's one there for you. "

"Thank you. I appreciate your kindness." She really did. He'd gone out of his way to invite her to an event even though he didn't know her and she'd only arrived less than twenty-four hours ago. "How about I bring a bottle of wine, then?"

Connor reached out, propping one hand on the window. "You don't have to. But if you do, I drink both red and white and will have glasses on hand." Withdrawing his hand, he reached up and pulled down the sunglasses she hadn't noticed until now. "See you then."

He walked away while she sat, quivering from the growing intensity of whatever strange emotions where dancing around in her gut.

In the rear-view mirror she watched as he got into his car, then with a jaunty wave drove away.

"Now that was interesting."

Kelly shook her head, started the car, rolled it forward then paid great attention as she backed out of the driveway.

~

Connor arrived back at his office still winded from the interview with the new teacher. She'd introduced herself as Kelly, and he realised he like the sound of it. As he entered his office, Penny was waiting, a wad of papers ready for signing.

"Penny, could you make sure I've got two red and two white wine glasses and a bottle opener ready for tonight? I'll also need two folding chairs." Without Penny's assistance, there was no way he'd be ready for the official council event that took place every year. Even if he weren't chairing the introduction, he would be busy for the rest of the day tidying up the necessary paperwork to ensure it went without a hiccup.

Penny glanced at him. "That was fast work."

He grunted, "It's not a date. She's just arrived and won't have anything ready. So don't start your matrimonial rot on me."

Penny laughed, having only married in the last six months to the owner of the hotel in town. Warren 'Wozzel' Nabston was a grumpy bear of a man in his mid-thirties but the motel was a hub in the township, with many a lost waif finding themselves invited to major holiday meals there when alone in town. He'd mentioned Kelly to Penny who'd made a point of telling Connor that she wouldn't know about tonight. Of course, in acting on the suggestion, he'd left himself wide open to all manner of speculation—such as it was in small country towns.

He snorted, grabbed the sheaf of papers she shoved in his direction, muttering, "there's nothing worse than the newly married for machinations, you know. Especially for those who aren't looking."

As he reached his new office door, he heard her call out, "that's what I said!"

He slammed the door, retreated to his office chair and sank down.

Certainly he'd like to get to know Kelly better, but if he read her half as well as he thought, she was wary of any kind of relationship. If he planned to pursue her, he'd need to take his time.

Having just agreed to a four-year contract time was on his side.

Banishing all thoughts of relationships, he opened the file and started working through the documents within.

By five, he was shutting down his computer and tugging at his tie, tossing it into his briefcase, so he wouldn't forget it when he headed home. The day had included a video-conference with a state minister and he was feeling the pinch of the more formal dress code.

He'd just unbuttoned the top two buttons of his shirt and rolled up his sleeves when a tap came at the door. Penny peered inside, grinning conspiratorially. "You have a visitor."

"Oh sure." He frowned wondering who it might be when Penny ushered Kelly in.

"I'm sorry I'm so early, but being late is the biggest bug bear for me. I hope you don't mind."

Penny grinned. "Don't sweat it. Country towns don't stand on ceremony." Connor knew she meant it, but Kelly blushed. "I'll pop these into the fridge until it's time to head outside." Penny raised the bag containing several bottles of wine for them both to see.

"It's all good." He grabbed his briefcase, tie slithering out and pooling on the floor.

"Let me." She bent quickly and a surge of heat filled his cheeks as he caught a glimpse of her cleavage down her light shirt.

Even as Kelly stood up he was retreating, knowing that acting now would undo all his work.

"Grab a seat or would you like to look around."

"Look Connor, I don't want to put you out. Honestly I wasn't sure where to go so thought the safest bet was to stick my head in the door, then Penny insisted I should come in." She spoke in quick urgent tones and it settled his ardour back to a cooler sizzle.

"Come on, then. I'll show you the chambers. It's not big, but well, it's mine."

"You're not the mayor though."

He didn't bother containing the laugh. "No, I'm the CEO." When she looked at him with a blank expression he explained, "the Chief Executive Officer."

"Oh!" She covered her burning cheeks. "I don't know a lot about Local Government, but I know you're in charge."

"Sort of." Connor ushered her through the door and across the hallway. "Here's the chambers." The room featured dark panelling, a long conference table with twelve chairs crowding the heavy wood top.

On the wall, rows of photographs frowned down, ranging from the dark sepia tones to the bright glossy images of more recent groups of councillors overseeing every decision of those who came after them.

"So much history in here."

His own gaze took in the view. "Yes, a long and very illustrious one. Now it's my responsibility to make sure the decisions we make are the best for the future of Heartbreak Hill."

When she turned, she brushed against his shirt, Kelly's eyes widening. "Oh yes. But everyone speaks highly of you."

"They're probably just being nice, you know." He spoke flippantly, uncomfortable discussing what they thought of him.

The air between them thickened, like molasses and he swallowed, her scent invading his senses.

The knock at the door broke the spell and they pulled away, like school children found in an inappropriate embrace.

"Connor, it's almost twenty past. You should head outside now. Take Kelly. And I've had the chairs and glasses you requested popped out there and a bowl with some ice for the bottles."

Thankful for the opportunity to escape the confines, he grabbed her hand. "Come outside with me and meet some people."

He towed her through the glass exit and beyond the gazebo where people were already gathering.

Kelly watched and listened through the speeches, the explanation of how Heartbreak Hill was settled in the later 1800's and heard about the privations they'd endured.

"The town would have died without the river and the mining boom, but when the miners left we had to reinvent ourselves," the mayor intoned, glancing down at the notes on his lectern. "But for all the years that have passed and the indignities we've witnessed, our community continues to exist clinging to the settlers code." A smattering of voices echoed his words, imbued with pride. It filled Kelly with warmth knowing that they still celebrated a culture that was slipping away in most sections of the communities she'd lived in.

"Tonight, we raise a glass to those who suffered and fought the elements. Those who went to war and returned and those who didn't. For the children who grew, married and raised their own families here in Heartbreak Hill. Without them, this lifestyle and our town couldn't continue to exist.

"To our history and our settlers."

The crowd echoed the toast, raised glasses then drank deeply.

Behind Kelly the heat of the day melted away, replaced by the cooling tingle of the sunset.

A small knot of children played happily, in the park on her left and with practice born of experience, she kept one eye on the behaviour while trying hard to ignore the visceral pull that had her gaze homing again and again on Connor.

He couldn't yet be thirty but here he was, running this council, interacting so easily with the community. She'd met Ferret, Nobby and Snake—all Councillors—along with Pook, Boofy, Bear and Froggy. She learned they were a mix of shearers or labourers with the Council and each passed a nudge or a wink at Connor.

I hope he doesn't get the wrong idea, she thought, then she snorted. She'd agreed to attend so she could meet others, not be introduced as his girlfriend, though it seemed more than a few entertained that view already.

Connor slumped into the seat beside her, hand hovering over the glasses and glanced in her direction. "Red or White?"

She'd taken the easy option of one of both, though her

preference leaned toward a nice cool chardonnay. "I prefer white."

He grinned and leaned in. "I prefer red."

"Then we'll each enjoy a glass and settle in for the movie."

Kelly watched Connor's deft movements, quick jerks that uncapped each bottle, the careful pour. When he handed her the glass, she almost gasped at the electric spark that flared where skin touched skin.

"Thanks." She couldn't help the huskiness in her voice and for a moment it seemed that his gaze sharpened and heat flared between them.

Connor raised his glass to her, she clinked it with her own then they each took a sip before settling in to enjoy the movie under the stars.

~

Morning came all too quickly, and Connor stared at the ceiling, wondering if Kelly had risen yet? The night before he'd worked hard to concentrate on the movie-a difficult quest with Kelly sitting beside him—at least he knew the themes of The Castle. By the end of the movie, his awareness of her teetered on the edge of hunger. Already the boys, Boof and Froggy were sniffing around her and if he didn't make a move, they'd muscle in. He needed to do something, lest she slip away. Funny, he'd never before thought himself to be territorial.

The phone jangled and he reached over.

"Connor Bao McElvery, you didn't ring last night." The thick Scottish accent of his mother centred him.

"No I didn't. Sorry Mum. It was the Back To Heartbreak Hill night. I thought I told you about that?"

"Oh you did. I just forgot in all the excitement." She sighed and Connor frowned.

"What's happened?"

"He asked. I said yes."

It took a moment for Connor to work out the cryptic clues of her words. It clicked and joy cascaded. "I'm so pleased for you both. You deserve to be happy mum."

He was. Having raised him by herself after her fiancée, and Connor's father, had died in the months before his birth, Connor had watched her work and worry herself as he'd grown up. The bond between them was exceptionally close and he had known Simon intended asking Niamh to marry him, but he hadn't given Connor a clue as to when he planned to pop the question. They'd spoken at least two months ago about Simon's plan, well before Christmas.

"Set a date yet?"

"No Connor. There's no rush." But there was a shadow of uncertainty in her voice.

"Mum, do you need me to—"

"No, Connor. I just... It reminds me of when I was engaged to your father. Losing him just before was hard. At least that time I had you." Her words died away and he contemplated telling her about Kelly.

The itch grew and he dragged in a deep breath. "Mum, I've met someone."

Silence grew.

"Mum?"

"Out there? A country girl?" An indefinable thread tugged at him.

"No. She's just moved here. She's nice. Her name is Kelly but I think she's had a hard time. She's gorgeous but..."

"You think she's running away from something? You've always been excellent at reading people, love."

"She accompanied me last night to the barbeque. I walked her home and we're going fishing this afternoon."

Niamh's laugh tinkled. "Such a romantic date."

"It's not a date, Mum. We're just going fishing." He knew his tone sounded defensive, but if he allowed himself to quantify the appointment as anything else, and nothing came to pass it would hit him far too hard.

His emotions, usually serene and settled according to his mother, were roiling like a mad sea leaving him sure that he teetered on the edge of something momentous.

"Offer to bait her hook for her. Most girls don't like doing that themselves."

"So that's the way to a girls heart?"

"Don't mock it Connor. Your father baited mine and I was his from that point on." Connor changed the topic, catching up on the news of the last few days then made an agreement to ring on Monday, he hung up considering the ceiling once more.

Bait the hook. If only it were that simple.

CHAPTER THREE

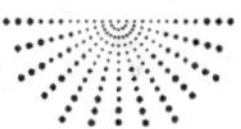

Kelly sat on the verandah, phone in hand as she gazed over the landscape she was rapidly coming to love.

Connor was due for dinner in under twenty minutes and she was a mess. The call from her solicitor had shaken her to her very foundation. "David's free."

The future she'd been carefully building since moving to Heartbreak Hill, the one where she'd restarted her life, found a joy in the simple things like fishing with Connor, going for walks or simply spending time cooking a barbeque now felt like a farce.

"How could this happen?" The numbness that had settled over her made movement next to impossible.

At least David didn't know where she lived and getting here would be a huge effort.

The sound of a car slowly inching up the road had her turning and the fear that she'd been so sure she'd thrown off swamped her. The car inching into her driveway was a white four wheel drive. *Connor.*

He would understand if she told him she didn't feel up to

tonight. Cowardly though the thought was, she did, for just a moment, considered shutting him out.

He closed the car door and advanced towards her, his long strides eating up the gravelled path and he carried two bottles of wine—a joking reminder of their first unofficial outing together.

When he caught sight of her face, his tightened, gaze narrowed and lips thinned. "What's wrong?"

She struggled to find the words, but the hot sting of tears burned. "I... I need to tell you about me, Connor. There's so much I haven't..."

Finding the words proved difficult, but he carefully stood the wine bottles on the small outdoor table and took her hands in his. The warmth of his palms scorched her frozen fingers and Kelly realised that in the time since the call, she'd chilled.

"Kelly, let me help you."

He would. He'd do everything in his power to keep her nightmares at bay she realised. The last six months of outings and dates had been marred by her inability to share her history with him. It was past time to rectify that.

"Connor, come sit down." She patted the chair beside the one she was perched in.

He settled and drew her close, an arm carefully slung over her shoulder so she could lean against him.

"I was married, Connor. David—my ex—courted me in a whirlwind: Flowers and movies, weekends away. I'd only known him a couple of months when he asked me to marry him. I was so sure. He seemed right on every level and I said yes. Before I knew it we were married. Then it all went wrong. He'd yell and scream that I'd ruined dinner. The dress I wore was wrong—too revealing— and all the men were looking at me. One day he hit me."

She dragged in a wobbly breath, hoping to find the

courage to tell him the rest. "It got worse. Six months into our marriage I knew I couldn't stay. His behaviour escalated so quickly and it was getting harder to hide the bruises." Kelly's voice broke but she went on.

"I tried really hard but knew if I stayed things would get worse. I'd seen battered women and knew the statistics. All my life I'd said things like, they should leave. Then that was me."

Kelly waited for Connor to release her, to speak but he didn't. It was as if he realised she needed to say the words she'd only ever spoken to the Counsellor. Not even her mother knew exactly what happened, just that Kelly had run.

"When I decided to leave, Mum and Dad came over. David was on a business trip. He's... He was an investment banker. We got my stuff and I moved into a rental unit. I filed for divorce and stupidly thought that was all it would take. The solicitor suggested a Domestic Violence Order but I was so arrogant because he hadn't found me so I ignored it. The receptionist sent my paperwork to the wrong address and he found out where I was."

"If it's too much, you don't have to tell me more." For a moment she wondered if he was ready to hear it all, then understood, he was giving her the chance to tell him every-thing. But the wound needed lancing and he had to under-stand if they had any possibility of a relationship.

"He found me. The police came. I moved and thought it was all okay. He found me again and followed me but I got away. I drove to the police station and he couldn't touch me. The last time was sheer bad luck. I was shopping in the mall and he saw me. It took two bystanders to pull him off but he'd already hurt me."

She tugged at her hair and pulled aside the straps of her frock, exposing to his view for the first time, the jagged scar.

"I'd kill him for you, Kelly." The words stabilised her.

"They jailed him for two years, with a non-parole period of eight months. I didn't realise until they rang me—the solicitors. He's out Connor and I'm afraid."

~

Anger bubbled deep in Connor's gut. This creature had hurt Kelly, not just physically but emotionally too, and that was unacceptable to him.

"He won't find you Kelly, and if he does he has to go through me and everyone in this town. The kids adore you, the parents would do anything for you. I would lay down and die for you." He spoke clearly, waiting for her to understand the importance of what he just said.

Now, with the knowledge of her background he thanked his ability to read people because if he'd ploughed in when the first thrust of interest had caught him unawares, he'd have no chance at winning Kelly. Simply put, anything other than forever with her wouldn't work.

He stood and tugged her up, into his arms. "You're an amazing woman Kelly Chester. An amazingly talented teacher, a beautiful woman and an awful fisher-person."

She laughed, a wet and snotty sound. "Wow, overwhelm me with compliments, why don't you?" Then she hiccupped, as tears began trickling down her cheeks.

She shook and he tugged her into a deep embrace. She needed to release those emotions to heal.

Minutes passed as the maelstrom built and crashed down on her, each sob and damp tear that soaked into his shirt adding to the fury that he struggled to contain. That this man had damned her to this damaged existence was against every point of morality.

Connor promised himself if the man ever darkened Heartbreak Hill, he wouldn't hold back.

Kelly wound her arms around his waist. "Wow, that was some way to welcome you, wasn't it?" She laughed thickly. and he rested his cheek on the top of her head.

"I wouldn't have you any other way, Kelly."

He rubbed his hands up and down one arm and frowned, noticing how cold she'd become.

"We should go inside, so you don't catch a chill."

"That's what I lo..." Kelly shook her head but not before he caught the gist of her words. She loved him, she just wasn't ready to accept it yet. While the threat of the danger David posed hung over her, she wouldn't allow them to forge a deeper more lasting relationship.

Once more his loathing of a man he'd never met overwhelmed Connor but he refused to allow his emotions to bubble over onto Kelly. She'd dealt with enough negativity and tonight he planned to make her smile and forget, even if just for a short time, the worries that harried her.

Instead, he herded her into the house and followed her, his gaze casting a quick glance across the road before closing the door.

Over dinner Connor worked at putting Kelly at ease, pouring her wine and clearing the table. The more he did, the more she felt ambivalent about their relationship—if she could call it that.

"Connor, would you sit down, please?"

He turned in her direction. "I just thought I'd wash up."

"No, sit down. I'll do that. I want to talk to you." She bit her lip wondering the best way to approach what she needed to say.

He sat down, wariness in the tensing of his muscles. "Okay."

"I think we should stop spending so much time together." She looked away, feeling the tension in the air between them.

"Why?"

Kelly clasped her hands together, fingers twining. "It's not fair to you that I can't and won't commit—"

"Rubbish." He spoke forcefully and for the first time she heard that hint of steel she'd always been sure lay beneath the surface.

"I beg your pardon?" She embraced every inch of the maiden aunt and schoolmarm attitude that she could muster.

"Don't speak rubbish, Kelly. You're afraid. I understand that. You're worried David will find you. That he'll hurt you." He leaned forward in his seat, so that his arms were braced on the dining table. "I understand that, but what I didn't take you for is a quitter and a scaredy-cat."

Anger bubbled away in her belly. "A scaredy-cat and quitter?" She spoke each word with a clarity that came with fury.

"Yes. You're afraid and I understand that, but if you choose to do it alone you shame me. You belittle us. That's not the Kelly I know and have come to adore. The Kelly who's strong and courageous, the one who faced a township she didn't know to share wine with me. The one who moved hundreds of miles to begin again. That's the Kelly I love."

Stunned, Kelly couldn't begin to formulate a rebuttal. He loved her? He'd never shown that.

She shook her head, trying to clear the haze that settled in her mind at those simple words.

"Please leave." The words tore from her mouth before she could stop them and he stilled, face settling into a hard as stone attitude.

"I'll go for now. But I'll be back."

He scraped his chair from the table and stood, eyes glittering with anger. "When I come back, I want you to have considered exactly what you're thinking of throwing away, because this isn't just about you anymore. This is about us."

He stalked toward the door and she reached out a hand, but he didn't look back.

Agony flared once he'd gone and the echo of the car engine died away while she laid her head on the table and sobbed.

~

On the floor the kitten Connor had ordered for Kelly played with the ribbon. His heart ached for her and even more for the way she'd thrust him aside.

Davina, the ragdoll, rolled and batted while Connor brooded.

His mother had delivered her this morning, bringing along Simon his soon to be stepfather. They'd gone to bed early when he'd headed off on the ill-fated dinner date, so here he was at nine o'clock at night wondering what do to with himself.

On a whim he picked up the phone and dialled Martin, his almost playboy best friend.

"Hey, I thought you had a hot date tonight, Connor."

"Yeah, well I guess it bombed because I'm home here with the kitten I had Mum collect for Kelly's birthday."

"Trouble in paradise? Something I can do to help?"

Martin had met Carrie this past summer, about the time he'd met Kelly and while Martin's path to true love had been both swift and stable, they spoke regularly about Connors slow courting of Kelly.

"She has an abusive ex-husband."

"Ahhh. Now we understand more. What are you going to do? Because whatever it is, you'll need to tread carefully," Martin summed up the angst he was dealing with.

"If only it were that simple... She threw me out." He speared his fingers through his hair, frustration eating at him.

"What do you need?"

"I don't know Martin. I just don't know how to help because it's not something I have any experience of. She's afraid he'll find her. Hurt her. He cut her before and it took two people to pull him off. He'd sliced her shoulder..."

"Her? I remember reading about that in the paper. She was in hospital for ages, but they jailed him, Connor. I remember reading about that too."

"He's out and it's eating her alive."

He looked up and saw his mother frowning at him. "Look, mum's up so I'm going to hang up. I'll ring you tomorrow, okay?"

"Any time, bro."

He disconnected and glanced to his mother.

"Time for a cup of tea and some talking I think, my boy." She padded to the kitchen, her tartan dressing gown reminding him of all the times they'd done this in the past.

"I don't know what to do, Mum." He slumped to the table while she rattled around in the kitchen.

"You love her then?"

"Yeah."

"I thought that might be the case when I picked up the kitten before coming out. I'd offer to talk to her but this is something you two need to work out. I won't interfere, but if you need something ask. I'll do everything in my power to help you."

She popped two teacups, the honey and a pot on the table.

"Now tell me everything."

He did, explaining the things Kelly had shared. The way she'd ordered him from his home and his parting words while she listened. Niamh reached over and took his hand in hers, rubbing the top of his hand with her thumb.

"You spoke from the heart but she's hurting and lost. In some ways, you'll need to start at the very beginning, as if you'd never met before. Many women in her situation don't talk after the fact about what happen in their relationships. They hide the details like dirty washing, hoping one day they'll wash away the scars. I would imagine she's told you things that very few have heard. Take heart, my son. Tomorrow morning, bright and early you take that baby in there," Niamh pointed to the kitten, "and wish her a happy birthday. Then you take it a day at a time until she can find herself again."

In silence he poured two cups of tea and they drank while he considered her words before she rose and headed back to bed.

He sat there for a long time before following her lead, gathering up the dozing kitten and carrying it down the hall with him.

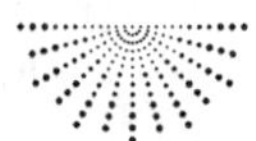

CHAPTER FOUR

"Crying yourself to sleep leads to puffy eyes," Kelly told her reflection then poked her tongue out.

On a sigh she cleaned her teeth, dragged a brush through her hair and frowned. *What will I do with myself?* Since Connor's mother and her partner were in town, they had planned to meet for dinner then watch a movie on the television. She guessed that plan had gone by the wayside.

The sound of the knock at the door caught her by surprise and she scurried in its direction. Swinging the door wide, she stilled. Connor stood there, a small cat carrier and a large paper bag in his hands.

"May I come in?"

She bit her lip, memories of the way she'd acted the night before washing over her. Shame coursed. "Connor. Please come in. I wanted to talk to you about last night. I said things I never should have uttered."

She hoped he'd stop and look at her but he gently laid the carrier on the floor then started to unfasten the door. "Come on cutie." He reached in and removed a bundle of white fluff.

"Connor?"

"Happy birthday Kelly."

He held out the kitten and she cupped her hand around the baby. It weighed almost nothing and stretched before stroking its tongue over Kelly's palm. "She's so beautiful! What's her name?"

"I played with calling her Davina. It's a Scottish name that means beautiful, but she's your kitten, so you should name her whatever you think is best."

She glanced up at Connor's face, before reaching up on tiptoes to kiss him on the cheek.

He started and the look of surprise on his face made her giggle, the kitten began to wiggle. "This is the best present anyone has ever given me. Thank you."

"I've got some other supplies here too." He indicated the bag.

"Well, I've never had a pet before so I'll need you to help me make sure I've got everything she needs."

"What? Never?" Shock echoed in his words and Kelly shook her head.

"We were never in one place long enough so it would have been cruel to move them all the time."

"Well, I'm glad it's me rectifying that then. Davina needs her litter tray filled up, a food bowl and water bowl. I've also got a bed and some toys. She's partial to them. Pop her on the floor and watch this."

Connor dragged out some ribbons and other cat toys and the furry, little bundle jumped and ran, ungainly sometimes but so energetically that Kelly laughed and clapped.

"She's had her first few shots, but will need worming and more boosters in a little while. Here's her immunisation folder."

The kitten settled herself on her bed and started grooming and Connor moved as if he were going to leave.

"Stay and have a coffee with me please? I'd really like to talk to you."

Kelly hoped he'd understand; she needed a chance to apologise for her behaviour.

He tilted his head. "You don't need to apologise." He framed her face with one hand, his thumb gently rubbing against her cheek.

She nuzzled in, needing the strength that came with his nearness.

"I was a coward last night. You hit the nail on the head and I didn't want to face the truth. I'm not a quitter though, even if last night it looked like I was. I'm not giving up on you or us. I... I want to see where this is going. I'm fairly sure I know where I stand, but I need time to make it happen."

His smile melted the cold bubble that had surrounded her. "I want that too, sweetheart. So, are we still good for tonight?"

"What about Davina?" His smile widened.

"Bring her along. I have a litter tray and food dishes at my place too, along with toys and a spare bed."

Her puzzlement must have shown.

"She can come have visits and still have everything she's used to there."

"Oh man! She's going to be the most spoilt kitty in Heart-break Hill. I'll just need to make sure she's okay through the day. I might come home at lunch and check on her." She gazed at the little white fluff ball now asleep on her bed, then rounded on Connor and threw her arms around her neck and kissed him. Full on the lips.

He stilled.

She stilled.

Oh. My. Word.

His lips opened and the kiss deepened, her body warming against his until dizziness dictated that she step away.

"I, uh..."

"Wow. Now that was something special." He grinned. "I'd better get out of here before my mother comes looking for me. Pop around say four o'clock and we'll settle Davina in and you can meet Mum and Simon. Or if you prefer I can pop over and pick you up?"

His brow quirked.

"I'll walk."

"It'll be cold for Davina. At least drive."

"All right. See you then, Connor."

When he left, she trailed him as far as the screen door and watched as he backed out of the driveway.

He cast a final look around. The steaks and satay kebabs were marinating in the fridge, along with the mix of salads already prepped. He'd also stashed a good white and a decent red, plus Simon's favourite beer in there too.

The table outside was set and Davina's dishes contained water and dry bits sprinkled over with a little fresh fish chunks.

"You've been busy, son." His mother laid her hand on his shoulder. They'd been out today visiting the local historical society, the old hospital and making the drive to Buccanoo with the lonely pub and cattle yards just over an hour away.

Connor turned and hugged his mother. "She's coming tonight and I wanted to make sure everything was in order."

Niamh nodded. "I'm pleased to see that. Now, what can I do for you?"

"I've taken care of most of it. I'm just going to shower and dress before she arrives. Can you keep an eye out? She's bringing Davina with her."

His mother laughed. "You and your pets. Go on. If she arrives I'll let her in and even pour her a wine."

He retreated, wondering if he could make it out before she got to the house. He didn't want her scared because his mother might be over the top with her meeting of Kelly.

Connor stilled at the bathroom door, closed his eyes. She'd never been heavy handed before with his girlfriends. He'd never been concerned that she might be too forward. Why was this time different?

He rested his head on the jamb. Because none had ever mattered so much before.

Rushing through his shower, he took the time to shave then dress in jeans and loose shirt, the first two buttons left open, then after quickly refreshing his breath he inhaled and headed for the lounge.

Kelly had arrived, her dress, a grey wool pinafore belted at the waist, with a light cotton long sleeved tunic of red was eye catching enough to look interesting yet reserved enough to be considered inoffensive. Her hair was tied back in a knot at the nape of her neck, and he ached to kiss her. With his mother and Simon there, and after last night and this morning, he was sure the ground was far too shaky for that, so, instead, he invited her to sit.

Kelly chose the side of the three-seater closest to him and Connor guessed he should be thankful for that. At least she hadn't perched on the other side of the lounge room in the armchair.

His mother settled next to Kelly and continued to pet on Davina, who, sure of her welcome, purred and kneaded at his mother.

"I take it Mum introduced herself and Simon?"

"Oh yes. She sent Simon to pour me a wine too." Kelly grinned in his direction then thanked Simon as he handed her a glass from the tray he carried.

"Nice little kitten you have there. We collected her from the breeder Connor chose and she travelled well from Brisbane."

Kelly blinked in Connor's direction. "How did you manage that?"

Connor hadn't really planned on explaining any of this to Kelly, but on the spot he shrugged. "My best friends girlfriends mum breeds them. You'd talked about a cat so I just thought, since it was your birthday and you were out here alone a little furry baby would be welcome."

"She is." His chest tightened as she glanced in the direction of the kitten.

As if reading Kelly's glance as a call, Davina bounced off Niamh's lap and toddled over to Kelly to settle in hers.

Niamh reached over and patted Kelly on the knee. "So, you'll need to bring Davina with you when you come to Simon's and my wedding in October."

Connor sat up straight in his seat. "You didn't say you'd set the date. When did you make that decision?"

"This afternoon Connor. Your mother and I aren't getting younger and we've decided sooner is better than later. Then we're going to China for our honeymoon. Your mum wants to tell your father's family in person."

Connor couldn't still the surprise that spurted through him. "My dad's family? But I thought they hadn't ever responded to your attempts to contact them?"

Niamh shook her head sadly. "No, but I want them to know what a fine young man you are and it feels right to finally close that chapter of my life."

Simon clasped Niamh's hand across the gap between their seats. "And I agree. Our time is beginning but your family and mine will be the same. It's the right decision."

Connor slumped back in his seat, considering Niamh and Simon's words.

In the past, he'd let his mother make all the effort when it came to contacting his father's family and now he realised for the first time, it was also past time for him to make an effort too.

~

Kelly hummed as she readied for bed. She'd thoroughly enjoyed her time at Connors. With a grin, she uploaded an image to her social media account and tagged her friends so they'd see.

Stella and Marie had been nagging for ages to see pics of Connor and up until now, she'd been leery.

'I think he's gorgeous and look at Davina! He's the most amazing man ever!" The picture of her and Connor holding Davina uploaded slowly as she made herself ready for bed.

It felt right to see them, the two of them and the little kitten.

Davina padded into the bedroom, her mouth widening with a huge yawn.

"Yes, come on then." Kelly leaned over and picked the tiny furball up and placed her on the bed. "You can share with me."

Then on a sigh, Kelly climbed in, sliding the small tablet onto the bedside table and turning off the light.

CHAPTER FIVE

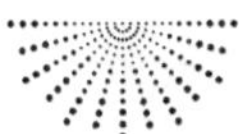

Kelly trudged home from work, knowing that she'd have to mark her way through the stack of books in her backpack was sobering. Friday evening and Connor not being home until tomorrow left her sighing.

"Okay, so you'll be alone tonight. It's not like you don't have experience in that." The problem was, in the last months, she'd come to enjoy the almost nightly visits from Connor or where she and Davina visited him. The conference on the Gold Coast had made travelling home today irresponsible and would have been dangerous. She felt far too deeply for him to ask Connor to even attempt it.

So she'd lay out the children's workbooks on the dining table, mark her way through the work they'd completed this week. Maybe watch one of the dvd's her mother had sent and curl up with Davina and a glass of wine.

Her phone pinged and she held it up, laughing at Stella's response to her photos. Lots of love hearts and a message. 'Seriously hunky Kelly. Keep him close by for a cold night.' Her laughter filled the air as she marched up the street, the weight of her bag forgotten.

At the give way sign, she turned right and stopped outside her house. In the window she could see Davina waiting and hurried up the driveway.

Unlocking the door, she shoved inside and the kitten came bounding over. "Have you had a good time, sweetie? Connor will be back tomorrow and we can both snuggle up on the lounge with him."

She curled her hands around the purring kitty and slid her bag onto the table.

"Right now I intend changing and—" the sound of her home phone jangled and she hurried over to answer it.

The line was silent and Kelly frowned. "Hello?"

Whoever it was clicked off their phone and the disconnect signal left her frowning. The ID had read "private", so she didn't know who could be calling.

Her skin crawled a little and a shadow of fear skittered through her, but Kelly reminded herself her number was also private. It couldn't be David. She's taken every precaution possible to ensure he wouldn't find her.

Besides, even if he had, the restraining order and the vast distance would beat him. He never liked travelling unless it was for work, so he wouldn't come out this far.

Kelly shook her head. "Come on Davina. Let's get changed, pour a wine and get started."

~

Connor stretched his shoulders hoping to release the stiffness in them from long hours of driving. Kelly had offered to make dinner, he still had to unpack his car and the small present he'd bought for her drew his gaze. The jewellers case lay on the seat beside him.

The tiny diamond cat necklace was just the thing. He'd seen it and it reminded him of Davina and the way Kelly had fallen in love with the little kitten. For that matter, he was sure Davina was sleeping in the spot he hoped to claim some time soon: beside Kelly. When he finally had her total trust and acceptance. Until then he was more than content—well, maybe not content, but at least resigned—to the status quo.

The sign Heartbreak Hill loomed and he grinned. "Doesn't seem to me to be too much Heartbreak right now."

His smile melted though, as he remembered the story recounted by a local guide filtered into his consciousness. The hill was so named after the original settlers had built around the tiny waterhole at the bottom of the hill. Within weeks tragedy had stuck when the hole became toxic with what they'd described as green slimy growth. Now they knew it as an green algal bloom. Almost fifty percent of the settlers, mainly children and older members had perished and were buried in the old cemetery out there.

As a result the township had moved to the running water a few kilometres or so from the original settlement.

"I should take Kelly out there one day soon, so she can see it." He nodded and determined that he would raise it with her tonight over dinner.

He turned into his driveway, thankful the house was at the end of the road nearest to the towns approach. He shoved out of the car and caught up his briefcase, before striding to the front door. Letting himself in, he was thankful the weather was cool; otherwise the house would be an oven. Unlike Kelly's traditional Queensland worker's cottage, which seemed to be snug in winter and cooler in summer, and built for the conditions.

Kelly. He wanted to ask her the most important question of all, yet he held back. After the debacle of her birthday three weeks ago, he refused to push forward on his plans to do anything official just yet.

She wasn't ready, even if he was.

He dumped the briefcase in his office and headed back out for the bags of groceries he'd picked up. He'd leave the cat food and litter they'd agreed he'd pick up for Kelly in the car along with the bottles of wine she'd asked him to purchase.

He did pick up the bottle of good quality French champagne, telling himself he wasn't living in a state of false hope. He wanted something special on hand for the day she said yes.

In his mind, a plan formed for how to propose. The only thing, in his mind, was the when.

The phone rang and he scooped it up. "Yes I'm home."

Kelly giggled. "I know. Nina was dropping off some books for me and said she'd seen your car in the driveway. So I thought I'd ring and remind you I said an early dinner."

Kelly enchanted him with her eagerness to spend time with him. Especially after a full week away attending meetings then a conference. The phone calls every night except last, weren't nearly enough for either of them. He wondered when that realisation would settle in her mind.

"I'm just unloading and I'll be on my way over."

"Excellent. Just don't forget the wine." Then without another word, Kelly hung up.

∼

Dinner was cooking, the scent of the country chicken casserole filling the air. Davina wound around Kelly's feet as she attempted to set the table. Bowls, glasses and cutlery sat in place as a knock came at the door.

Throwing it open she grinned and flung herself at him. "I've missed you Connor. I'm so pleased you're home."

With eager hands she tugged him inside. "In two weeks,

the kids are on vacation, my folks are heading out here and we should make some plans."

"I was thinking about that too. You asked me about the name Heartbreak Hill. I thought on the first Sunday, after your folks arrive we could maybe take a drive out there. It's quite an interesting location, not that I would suggest a picnic there, but we could head to Ganbulayunga."

"Where?" It was the first time she'd heard of the place.

"It's a pub, about fifteen kilometres from Heartbreak Hill and they serve the best counter meals. That is, if you'd like to go?"

Kelly glanced at Connor and nodded. His eyes were twinkling and warmth surged through her at the thought of just the two of them away from town for several hours. Heartbreak Hill was great, but the small township was also full of interested individuals, all willing to give them the benefit of their romantic experience.

"I'd love to Connor."

He set the bottles on the counter just as the phone rang. With a sigh Kelly reached out and picked it up. As before the line was silent and even though she said, "hello," several times it continued until the disconnect signal buzzed in her ears. Kelly frowned at the strange occurrence.

"Kelly? What's wrong?" Connor stepped up to her, his eyes roving over his face as if discomforted by what took place.

"It's no one. The strange thing is, this has occurred a couple of times now."

"Just be careful. There's a lot of scams currently doing the rounds. Or it could be one of those robo-calls some telemarketers make. It's hard to know what could be causing it, but likely nothing to worry about."

She nodded but the feeling of unease wasn't so easily

dismissed until Connor took her in his arms and kissed her, the feeling of being together, of touching, left her breathless.

She backed away, gripping onto the counter for dear life when he released her. Her chest pounding as the ever-present arousal curled in her stomach. She wanted him so badly and it amazed and humbled her that Connor was allowing her to set the pace of their relationship.

"Connor, I know you're waiting for me to give the okay for anything more between us. I appreciate it." She gave him a wobbly smile and the heat flared again in his eyes.

"I'm not interested in a quick steamy roll, Kelly. I want us to really connect. To form a deep and lasting union. I'll give you as much time as you need."

The deep hunger of his voice made her shudder with need as did the intensity of his words. "I'm trying, Connor." And she was. She'd accepted the fact that he'd do anything for her. That he'd wait until she was ready, even though on a purely physical level she had been there almost since they'd met.

His hand cupped her face. "When you're ready, you'll know."

She bit her lip realising that he'd ignore his own needs to ensure hers were met. Did that make her foolish or weak? Unable to answer that she nuzzled the palm of his hand then moved away, grabbing up the bottles of wine in a bag. "Thank you for bringing these. Let me pour us both a drink. Dinner shouldn't be long."

They'd planned an evening together, he would share the results of his time away and Kelly would regale him with the funny kids stories she'd amassed while he was away.

"I tracked down my father's brother this week." Connors words echoed and Kelly stilled, let the import of his words sink in then turned.

"That's fantastic Connor. How did you find him?"

"I have this friend who is great on social media. He managed to track him down. He's a business man in Hong Kong. Speaks English and Mandarin. I was pretty amazed when Zoe emailed me on Thursday."

"You've known since Thursday?" A little seed of sadness must have echoed in her words because Connor frowned.

"I needed a little time to consider what she said. Besides, I wanted to share it with you face-to-face. I'm thinking I should go to China soon. Meet them in the flesh. Mum tried hard to keep the lines of communication open, but my grandparents refused all contact and I'd like to know more about my history when we..."

Connor shook his head. "It's going to sound like I'm putting the cart before the horse. We can discuss this later."

"No, Connor. Tell me what you're thinking, please."

"The Chinese part of me is something I haven't ignored, but until now haven't really considered to be an essential part of who I am. I mean, mum would drag me along to language classes and cultural days. She encouraged me to meet with other children from Chinese families, but I never really connected or saw myself as part of that bigger culture. As I got older, she let me decide if I wanted to continue and I never bothered with it. I mean I'm Australian, right? But now, with you, I need to know more. If—when—we take the next step, talk about kids, I want them to know about their heritage. Both sides."

His words fed the yearning that she'd hidden deep within her psyche. The one that said forever, families and children. It stole her breath.

"Kelly, when I go there, to Hong Kong and China, I want you to come with me."

Oh God! Was this it? Was going to ask now? Giddiness hit then passed as he scooped up his wine and sipped it, leaving her empty.

"You're not saying much." His hands shook and she understood. He wasn't ready to ask her the question, but was testing the ground. He needed her to respond one-way or the other. He was asking if there was hope for more.

"I... I'd like that Connor. When you're ready." Her answer sounded wimpy to her but it was the best she could manage under the circumstances.

CHAPTER SIX

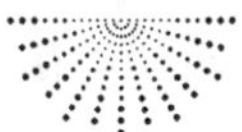

Connor waited until midday, knowing that her parents were due to arrive in the afternoon. He didn't want to wait, the urge to talk to Kelly's father and seek his approval clawing at him.

His mother already knew his plans. He'd take Kelly to the mountain, show her what remained, then bam! Pop the question. Checking his watch again, he smiled, scooped up the keys and headed out of the house.

His car, washed for the occasion, his best jeans and an open collared shirt. He'd paid extra attention to shaving hoping to stave off the worst of his nervousness.

The car almost steered itself as he drove to Kelly's house. He cleared his throat, wiped damp palms over the legs of his jeans and climbed out.

Kelly's house door opened and a large man, barrel chested and shoulders like a footballer wandered out of the house, down the steps and met Connor by the car.

"You must be Connor?" His gravelly voice raked him, the nerves he battled to control making him more than a little fragile.

"Yes I am, Mr Chester. Thanks for meeting with me beforehand."

"My pleasure. She's told you about David?" The gaze of the ex-policeman zeroed in and Connor nodded.

"Yes. She told me about the attack, the speed of their relationship. How he treated her. I promise not to do that. She's a good person who didn't deserve any of what came before, but it's my job to make sure that the rest of her life is as near to perfect as I can make it. I'll make her happy."

"You already have. Come on in and meet my wife, Sian. That cat you got her? Davina, she's mad. The minute we entered she's crawling all over us. Never seen such a thing."

"Davina is spoiled. I have to admit, she's got toys at both our houses, beds, food bowls. Even my mother has bought some for when we plan to go down to visit. I'm thinking Christmas would be a good time to visit both families."

Ted Chester—Kelly's father—nodded. "I agree. You'll want to make a visit down afterwards, even if it's just a flying run, but Christmas will be an excellent time to make decisions and work with both families."

The entered the door and Kelly pierced him with a 'what's going on' look.

"I found him outside loitering. Thought I should take pity on him, Kel. Now Sian, this is Connor."

He leaned in to shake hands when the woman flung her arms around him, tugging him close for a hug and a wet kiss on his cheek.

He grinned at Kelly, knowing she'd have no idea why he was so pleased. Once Sian released him, he moved to Kelly, laid a gentle kiss on her lips and gloried in the sensation of her melting against him. An imperious meow ended that and everyone laughed as Connor reached down to lift the half grown cat into his arms. "Yes, hello to you too, Davina!"

~

Sunday morning found Kelly in the four-wheel drive that Connor usually drove, heading out to Heartbreak Hill. Her parents had decided to stay at home to look after Davina —their one and only possible grandchild as Sian had stated— and rest.

It took a lot for Kelly to realise that her parents were growing older and the drive, fifteen hours of it, allowing for the necessary fuel and toilet stops, had left them tired. At least, with two weeks resting at Kelly's before heading for home, they'd be well refreshed.

Kelly shook her head and re-focused on the road ahead. In the distance, the hill rose like a red blob against the mainly plain landscape.

"I can't believe you've not had the opportunity to come out here. You've been in Heartbreak for nearly nine months."

"Well, the first couple of months were pretty busy, settling in, organising my timetables and working out my teaching schedule. Then you and I started to spend a lot of time together. When I went back to Brisbane in June it was for Stella's wedding, so no chance to go anywhere then." She shrugged. The year had passed incredibly quickly but with that came the very real concern that her contract at the school was originally for one year. Something she hadn't actually shared with him.

"Connor, you know I'm here for a set period, right? I only had a contract."

Connors hands turned white on the steering wheel. "Are you trying to tell me you're leaving?" His voice sounded strained and Kelly reached out touching his left hand. It flinched and Kelly frowned.

"No! I mean, I've requested an extension to my contract but it was only for a year. It's been indicated, that as the Principal is happy with me, the likelihood is they've give me another year here. But until the paperwork is settled, I can't be totally sure." She leaned in. "I'm not keeping anything from you, Connor. Total honesty was lacking in my marriage to David and I need us both to be open."

He nodded and continued driving, the rough road having them bouncing up and down, a plume of red dust rising behind them, while emus rushed past.

When they finally drew to a stop, Kelly sat, looking over the imposing rise, the remains of houses littering the ground. Behind the hill she caught sight of the water source.

"This is where the settlers first came to Heartbreak Hill. It was called Harmony, because the settlers thought they'd found the garden of eden almost. The ground here was covered in green grass hiding the rocky terrain. The cattle yards were over there," Connor pointed to a couple of lonely sticks still protruding from the ground. "Fifty people perished here in the first year, with forty-seven making the move to what is now known as Heartbreak Hill. They were committed though, to making it work out here. They brought their families and everything that was important to them. Imagine the wagons lurching as the children clung to the sides, Kelly. The hope that they'd reached a better land, one where freedom wasn't just an idea but a reality."

Kelly could see it. She carefully stepped around the forgotten remains of the township, hand shielding her eyes as she searched the ground. At the bottom of the hill, Kelly found a toy, half buried in the dirt.

"Look what I found Connor. A toy." He hunched down beside her.

"Imaging the look on the child's face when their father or mother handed them this little metal wagon." He scratched it out with his fingers. "I wonder if he had to promise something before they gave it to them. Kelly?" His voice deepened and Kelly glanced at him, then the hand he reached out to her.

She rose, her stomach erupting in a mass of fluttering butterflies.

"Kelly, I love you and I know you love me. I promise to never hurt you, let you down or make you feel the need to run. I pledge my entire life to making you feel like the princess you are. Marry me?"

Out of his jeans pocket he tugged a box, small and covered with dark blue leather. Flipping open the top he showed her a beautiful emerald ring. She reached out. "My hands are dirty."

Tears flowed down her cheek. He'd set this up, to show her that the first promise might not always work, but through hard work, acceptance of loss, there was always hope. Just like the history of Heartbreak Hill.

"Kelly, I don't care if they're dirty, put me out of my misery. Yes or No?"

She giggled at the frustration in his voice. "Yes, Connor. I will marry you." He kissed her on the lips, hard and hungry. When he stepped away, dizziness assailed her. She barely felt him sliding the ring on her finger until he covered it with his lips and kissed it in place. "This is a symbol of my promise, Kelly."

~

Kelly washed her hands in the pubs sink. The morning had passed in a haze after the proposal and glancing down, she still couldn't believe he'd asked her like that.

It had been perfect. With David there'd been flowers, a romantic dinner and dancing, but it was as empty and shallow as him. With Connor, there was substance.

Excitement welled and Kelly hurried out to the main bar

where Connor waited, sipping on a coke. They'd wait 'til they were back at Connor's before celebrating. He promised fine French champagne and she'd wondered once more just how long he'd been planning this.

She settled into the seat beside him, his arm winding around her shoulder.

"Let's get a photo. Something for posterity."

He laughed and agreed. Kelly held up her phone making sure the ring was front and centre in the photo and snapped it once, another then a third. "In case the first two don't work."

A miniscule signal showed on her phone. "Can I share this do you think?"

Connor grinned. "I told my mother and Simon last night. I spoke with your Dad and he was telling your mum after we left this morning."

Kelly sputtered. "They all knew?"

"Well, I didn't want to propose with your Dad hanging over me. He's a scary man, Kel."

She laughed feeling the lightness of the moment. "Okay, so I can post it on Social Media." She took a moment and tagged her friends in the image and Connor too, along with the post, 'Guess what I got asked today?'

Then she settled in against his arm. "Was that what you were talking about yesterday afternoon when my Dad met you in the driveway?"

Connor nodded and she felt the movement. "Yeah. I wanted it done right. I wanted him to approve and know I am committed to you in every way possible."

"So what happens next?"

He spun her in his arms. "We set a date, plan for Christmas to be when you order your gown, flowers and arrange the wedding."

"I want a white one if you're okay with that. Last time, it

was rushed so my parents and Stella were there and his family but that was about it. We were married in the registry office and went out to dinner afterwards. It didn't feel wedding-like." She shrugged. "I want to share our happiness with everyone, Connor. This time it's forever and I want everyone to know and join us."

"Then that's what we'll do. Either here or on the coast, I don't care, so long as you turn up and we both say 'I do.' That's what matters most to me."

CHAPTER SEVEN

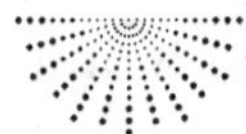

Kelly settled in the lounge, the first of the wedding magazines she'd ordered littering the chair around her. Thank heavens her mother collected the mail before they left this morning to head back to the coast.

Her mobile rang, she checked the name. Stella.

"Hey Stel, what's happening?"

"Oh God, Kelly. You're going to kill me. I'm so sorry." Anxiety flowed in waves from the phone.

"What's wrong Stella? Have you decided you don't like green for the bridesmaids gowns? Or have you ordered me some wild bridezilla pack—"

"It's worse, Kelly. I commented on the ring pic and tagged Alicia, Carly and Sarah."

Kelly nodded remembering the excited comments. "I saw that. So what's the problem?"

"David is still on Carly's friend list and he saw it." Kelly froze, hearing Stella say the words *he saw it.* She knew how dark his temper was and gulped audibly.

"What happened?" Davina jumped on her lap as if sensing her sudden fear, rubbing up against Kelly's arm.

"Carly said he contacted her last time when I tagged her in photos of you. Up until now though, while he'd asked for your phone number which she handed out..." Kelly almost stopped breathing at that, realising that those hang up calls had likely been David.

"After your engagement though I tagged them on your ring picture. That's when he contacted her again. You hadn't said anything about warning her and I didn't mention your business to her, so I guess she didn't know all the facts. About his behaviour and the abuse and why you divorced him. When he asked for your address she shied and just gave the name of the town thinking that should make him back off. She did ask him why he wanted it though, I guess because she was wary that if you hadn't given him your address and phone number that maybe there was something dodgy. David said he was sending something special to you." Stella sniffled down the line. "I'm so sorry Kelly. It didn't even occur to me to tell her to say nothing and now Carly's in a mess after I yelled at her. I should have warned her, but it just didn't occur to me!" Stella's voice rose in anguish and Kelly wasn't quite sure how to respond.

"I..." nausea rose and it took Kelly a moment to battle it back. "I'll ring you back. I need to talk to Connor."

Kelly disconnected the line, hands shaking and it took a number of deep breaths before she could press the button to find him on the contact list.

The phone rang once, twice then he picked up. "Hey sweetheart, I'm in the middle of—"

"David saw the engagement post, Connor."

She knew the instant the words connected with his brain. "How?"

"Stella tagged some friends and he saw it. He said..." She gulped again, the words sticking in her throat.

"Stay there, I'm on my way." The line went dead and Kelly choked on a sob then rang her mother.

"Mum, David saw the post. Stella tagged Carly and apparently she's still friends with him. He's asked for my address. Can you get onto the solicitors? Connor's on his way over."

"Are you okay, Kelly? Do you need your father and I to..."

"No. It's all good mum. I just wanted you to know in case he turns up there. I don't think he has your address, just keep an eye out, okay? You know what the psychologist said at his hearing."

"I do. You'd be better staying at Connor's for the next little while and making sure Davina is safe too."

She nodded.

"Kelly?"

Of course! Mum can't see me! "Sorry mum, I was nodding, trying to think through everything."

"I know. If you need anything, your father and I are here to help you."

Kelly swiped at the tears streaking down her cheeks. "Thanks mum. You're the best."

The sound of the car door and hurrying footsteps had Kelly rising from her seat and she wasn't surprised when Connor pushed the door open and stepped into the room. He swooped her up in his arms, pulling her tight against him, so that Davina squeaked at the treatment.

"Get some clothes and whatever you need together. I'm going to move you into my place while we sort things out." Connor looked like some ancient warrior, his face grave and the muscles under his work shirt rippling.

Kelly shoved Davina into his hands. "I'm not sure that's the best..."

"You told me what he did last time, Kelly. I won't let him hurt you again. Get your stuff."

He sounded gruff and she knew it was all concern for her.

She could argue, but honestly she was terrified he'd find her or even worse Davina and make her pay, so Kelly whirled around, and hurried for the bedroom.

"Where's Davina's carrier?" Connors voice floated from the lounge room. By unspoken agreement they'd never yet entered each other's bedrooms, well aware that the temptation might prove too much. They may be engaged and Kelly may have been married, but they'd somehow come to an agreement that the final intimacy between them should be after their wedding.

"In the laundry. On top of the drier."

Kelly snatched up the suitcase on top of her wardrobe and began throwing in a mixture of clothing, enough for a week or two, making sure there were work clothes and relaxation choices too. Her hands settled on the lacey lingerie she'd bought and hadn't yet worn since her divorce and sighed, shoving them to the back of the drawer. *Not yet.* She would remove the tags and pop them into her case for the honeymoon, that thought drew a small smile, warming her enough to help fight off some of the chill which had settled in her bones.

Next, Kelly scurried to the bathroom, seeking the essentials of toiletries and makeup. She shoved them in her bag and pushed it down so it would zip up.

Tugging it off the bed proved a trial but she refused to bother him, knowing Connor was attending to Davina's needs.

Once off the bed, she dragged the suitcase, the wheels rattling on the wooden floors and popped it beside her couch. Into her briefcase went the marking she'd left on the dining table, charger for both computer and phone. She scanned the seat and gathered up the wedding magazines and slid them into the bulging side pocket.

Last, she collected the photos of her parents from the

television stand, her watch and handbag. Connor watched her with a hooded gaze. "Ready?"

Kelly nodded. "Yeah. Let's get out of here."

Connor scooped up her suitcase and Davina. You get the door and I'll take care of everything else.

Kelly swallowed, knowing her life had irrevocably changed once again.

~

Connor brooded. Kelly would be safe enough for now, having been dropped off at the library—Jane the librarian would be there along with the reading group ladies. It wasn't much protection, but he seriously doubted her ex would try anything inside a library filled to the brim with little old ladies, particularly with a ton of books in their bags. In his mind he tried hard to make light of his concerns.

They'd swung past the police station to apprise the sergeant, Kelly had contacted her solicitor and they'd started the paperwork to put the Domestic Violence Order in place, though, given what Stella had from Carly, and she'd sent a screen shot of Carly's garbled apology for passing on that Kelly was in Heartbreak Hill, he doubted there was much they could do. "There's no implied threat in the comments. We'll put the paperwork together, but I don't think it will fly, Kelly."

She'd looked so worried and pale it had taken every ounce of will power to drop her off. He'd rather be at home with her, but the pre-election education session for intending candidates couldn't be postponed. Instead of protecting the woman he loved, he was stuck here trying to share information about the role of a councillor.

The mayor, Frank, noted his abstraction. "Connor, what's wrong?"

Connor inhaled. "Kelly's ex-husband found out where she is. He abused her, attacked her and she was in the hospital for a while after he stabbed her in Brisbane."

Frank's brows drew together. "Is she in danger? If so, you should go."

Connor shook his head. "Not immediately so, but I have a bad feeling. He's worked out she's in Heartbreak Hill and I'm worried he'll come looking for her."

Frank clasped him on the shoulder. "Get us a photo and everyone in town will keep an eye out for him. She's safer here than in any big city. When we close ranks, nothing and no one gets through."

Connor settled back in his seat considering Frank's words. Maybe if he spoke to Kelly, she might have a photo of David, or her parents might. He scoffed. Maybe they were just making it into something more than it really was. He wasn't one to cry wolf. But the itching at the nape of his neck continued, worrying at him through the meeting.

At four o'clock, when the attendees filed out of the room, Penny met him at his desk. "Leanne from the post office said there's a parcel for Kelly, but since she wasn't at home she's dropped it off here."

Connors gut churned and he turned and marched into his office. "Call the sergeant and ask him if he'd pop on over. Also get a message to Kelly, she's at the library and ask her if she'd pop in too. I need to see both of them."

On his desk sat a large box, wrapped in cling film with fragile stickers attached. The handwriting on the top simply read, 'Kelly Chester, C/- Post Office, Heartbreak Hill.'

It could be from David or there could be another explanation. He could be clutching at straws or it could be something far more serious.

When the sergeant, Victor entered his office, Connor was perched on his office seat still eyeing off the package.

"You needed to see me?"

Connor indicated to the box. "This arrived for Kelly. No actual address, just care of the post office. I wasn't game to touch it or open it."

"Does Kelly know?"

"I'm waiting for her to arrive, Victor. My brain says there's nothing good in here. I hope I'm wrong, though."

Victor settled into the chair opposite Connor. "Well, we can't open it until Kelly arrives as it's addressed to her."

They waited in silence and five minutes later Kelly let herself into the office, her face turning pale as she spied the package. "Is it from him, Connor?"

Victor stood in unison with Connor and approached Kelly. Connor wound his arms around the shaking woman and pulled her closer.

"I'm sorry Kelly, but I need to know if you recognise the handwriting?"

She looked down then jerked back as if burned. "Yes. It's David's."

Kelly spun away, grasping onto the sleeve of Connor's shirt.

"We should open it." Victor glared at him across the room as he advanced on the package, tugging on latex gloves. "Don't want my fingerprints on it, even thought, seeing as it's come through the mail there's likely dozens." He withdrew a small multi-tool from his pocket and sliced through the clingy film surrounding the box.

He hissed, leaning away from it and sighed. "Not a nice boy at all."

Connor disengaged himself from Kelly and stared into the box, as Victor tugged aside the bubble wrap. Inside lay a couple of CD's, smashed into large cracked chunks, a package containing a hammer and some photos. They were daubed with red and Connor felt sickened. It was clearly

Kelly and some guy. "Wedding photos," he muttered and Kelly jerked convulsively at his words. When she made to turn, he held her still. "No, you don't need to see, sweetheart."

Victor sighed. "You should talk to your solicitor but I doubt there's enough here for a protection order."

~

Kelly felt the waves of frustration and anger rolling off Connor. "I don't have to stay here if it makes things difficult, Connor. I could go back—"

"What?" He swung around to pin her with a cold glare and she shivered. "Dammit Kelly, I'm not angry with you." He slid his arm around her waist as they walked to his house. "You didn't ask for this cretin to stalk you. All you did is get on with your life. We'll sort this out. Make sure he's locked up before he can do you any harm, so stop saying you'll go home by yourself. I won't get any sleep worrying about you and since my house is brick with security screens, it would be harder for him to get in. Makes me feel way more comfortable knowing you're in a secure house."

She sighed. "I'm not a wimp you know. I just don't get why he's so fixated on me."

"What did the psychologist tell you at the hearing."

Kelly hung her head, knowing she'd told him this before and that he was right. "She said in her view, he probably suffered from Antisocial Personality Disorder that caused him to be aggressive, to lie, to disregard authority and feel no empathy. That he'd feel no remorse and likely would consider himself the wounded party when arrested."

"So, are you to blame?"

His words stopped her in her tracks and he jerked to a halt beside her. "Why would you even ask that?" Hurt bloomed but he shook his head and clamped her to his side when she tried to squirm away.

"Listen to my question. Were you to blame?"

"No!" Anger flared and he smiled.

"See?"

It took a moment then she recognised what he'd asked and she shook her head. "No. It's not about me. I was merely the object he wanted and in his mind he owned me. I got away. The violence and behaviour is about him."

"Exactly. So we deal with this. And when it's done, we get on with organising our wedding. And in the meantime, we need to work out when because I'm thinking we'll take our honeymoon in Hong Kong and China. Seems to me it would be the right time to follow up on my grandparents. Does that suit you?"

"Yeah. It does. And I'm sorry I got angry with you." She was, truly. She could argue it away with the stress of David's reappearance in her life but it was frustration that one part of her life, the bit she'd tried hard to deal with kept rearing its head and biting her. Even after she'd done everything she could to set it right.

"When did you say the solicitor would ring you?" Connor's voice intruded into the fog of introspection and she shook her head. "Monday at eleven. In the middle of school lunch. I can take the call in the office while the TA's are on playground duty."

"Okay, Victor suggested if you have a photo of David we should share it around, so the guys on the road gangs will be keeping an eye out along with the shop keepers and Wozzel, in case he turns up."

"I hate plastering this all around town." However, her grumbling was weak.

"I know. But we do what we can, deal with the situation then go from there." They reached the gate and he swung it wide, allowing for her to enter the yard and up the steps to the door. Unlocking the door, he ushered her inside before locking it again.

Previously they'd have just pulled the door too and her heart bled at the realisation that because of David's actions Connor had to change a practice that had become familiar. It hurt and the tears that seemed to be constantly near the surface rose again. She sniffed as Connor pulled her close, kissing the top of her hair. "Come on, let's find Davina and have some family time."

She laughed a wet snotty sound as the cat loped into view with a meow. "Sounds good to me."

CHAPTER EIGHT

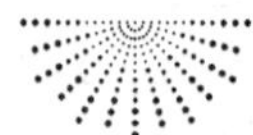

Kelly sat at her desk, the children having been released for the day. Friday afternoons were usually her favourite time of the week. Not because she left the town, but it meant two whole uninterrupted days with Connor and Davina. But right now, even that was overshadowed by the mess of her personal life.

The sparkling ring on her finger caught her gaze. Everything had changed when she'd accepted him.

The last term of the school year had begun slowly, staying with Connor had reinforced for Kelly that the decision to marry him and join her life with his was the right one.

There were only two flies in the ointment. The first and most pressing was David. In the last week Connor had put an answering machine on her home phone, checking in daily to see if there were any more hang up messages. Clearly it had been David, she now knew.

The second issue was the wedding and the intimacy they both hungered for and denied themselves. They'd agreed to abstain until they were married but it was like living in a pressure cooker. Every day the yearning to be closer gnawed at her mind.

Right now, she'd be happy with a small church wedding in Heartbreak Hill, the flowers delivered by her parents and the gown she'd seen online. The thought bloomed larger in her mind.

Gathering up her belongings, Kelly hurried toward her car. Connor had insisted that she should pop into the office every afternoon so he could be sure she was okay. Today, another thought sat uppermost in her mind.

The car beeped and Donna, the cleaner called out bye to her as she climbed inside the small blue sedan. Clicking the seatbelt into position, she pulled out of the parking lot and headed down the road to Connor's office.

Even as she parked, climbed out and locked the door ideas and plans came to mind. Penny, filling in at the reception counter waved her in. "You look like a woman with a plan."

"Oh I am. Is Connor free at the moment?"

Penny glanced at the phone system. "Yes. Go through, but he's got a meeting with Frank in about fifteen minutes."

"Awesome." As if on wings, Kelly hurried to his office, but stopped at the doorway, watching him reading through a document. "Ahem."

He lifted his head and winked at her. "I have an idea." She shut the office door and watched as he put the document on his desk. "I know I wanted a white wedding. We'd talked about near my parents sometime next year, but I have a new one, since we haven't actually planned any dates yet. How about we get married here on the second weekend of the school holidays. I mean, I know it's close to Christmas but everyone could come here. Wozzel said they're not normally busy then and Penny could check it. I've seen a gown. Mum could bring the flowers and Kev at the pub could cater or we could bring someone in. I don't want to wait, Connor."

She clasped her hands and leaned in as he stared at her. "But that means you don't have time for all the fripperies and girl times you missed last time, sweetheart. I want you to have the perfect wedding."

Kelly nodded enthusiasm urging her on. "I know, but we can have the perfect wedding here, Connor. My parents and I can stay at my place along with the bridesmaids. Stella and Marie are the only ones I want. You said Martin would stand up for you and he and your family could stay at your place. Or we could have your mum and my mum and the girls at mine and the guys at yours. What do you think?"

His smile banished her concerns. "Okay, if we can get everything done in time. Your dress?"

Kelly sighed. "I'd have to go to Brisbane but I've seen one and I know where it's available. If I head there next Friday, flying out on the Friday afternoon plane, I can shop Saturday and be home by Sunday morning. I can also arrange all the things like flowers, invitations etc. then."

"Jane at the library is an amateur photographer, and won a few prizes. If we can't find a photographer to come here, then we could ask her."

Then plan was coming together smoothly. "So, we're good to do this then?"

"Yeah sweetheart. It's going to be frantic but if you're sure there's enough time, let's go for it."

A squeal of joy split the air as Kelly jumped up and ran around Connor's desk to embrace him. "I promise it will be the best wedding ever!"

Bubbling over with joy as he tugged her closer her body began the slow burn that she associated with Connor.

The tap on the office door had her moving away, tripping

over her feet and landing on her bottom. The door opened just as Connor helped her to her feet.

"I thought it was Connor's job to go down on his knee. Am I interrupting?" Frank chuckled at his joke and Kelly grimaced.

"I'm just heading out. I'll see you at home." The words were softly spoken but carried an added promise as she skipped through the door, stopping by Penny. "Could you and Wozzel check the second weekend of the school holidays and maybe pencil out all the rooms?"

Penny stared at her. "That weekend? Here in Heartbreak Hill? We'll make it happen. You tell us what you need and if Wozzel and I can't do it, we'll find a way to make it happen."

Kelly scurried for the door hurrying as the sound of Penny's mobile pealed.

A hand, large and meaty intercepted her and before she could even yelp, she was silenced.

"Thought you could get away from me, you bitch!" He hammered her across the face with a meaty fist, before dragging her backwards.

Her mind awash with hazy pain but she fought to retain consciousness, knowing that this time it wouldn't end well for her.

~

Connor indicated Frank to sit down when Penny came screaming into his office. "Wozzel just called and David is here. He checked in this afternoon then took off when he challenged the guy. He headed in this direction. I just looked out and Kelly's car is there but no sign of her."

His heart stopped beating. Pain radiated from his chest before he was up and on his feet. "I'll call Victor. Penny can you alert the road gang via the radio. She's only just left. He can't have got her out of town yet, if that's his plan."

He dug out his phone, pleased that Victor was on speed dial and waited, heart in throat for him to pick up.

"Sergeant—"

"He's here and taken Kelly. Just now. From the Council office."

Shoving through the door, he stared at her heavy book laden bag lying beside it. "God damn it! Her bag is here."

"Connor, wait I'll be there in a moment."

Connor scanned the area, wide-eyed, blood pumping as the sound of a low guttural growl alerted him to danger nearby and all rational thought fled.

With careful strides, he stepped to the corner and peeked around the edge of the building. He dropped the phone to the ground, ignoring Vincent's directions.

The sight that met his graze froze his blood. A soft but obviously furious man was spitting words at Kelly while she stared at him glassy eyed.

"You shouldn't have left me Kelly. You're mine. You might have got a piece of paper that says you're free, but that doesn't count. *You're mine.*"

His fingers scrabbled at Kelly's hand. Connor wanted to jump on the man, but the large knife in his fist gave him pause. If he acted wrong Kelly would be hurt, and he'd do anything to avoid that.

A silent but flashing light caught his attention and he watched as Vincent pulled up to the curb, finger to his lips telling Connor to remain silent.

Vincent grabbed him by the sleeve of his shirt, remaining out of sight of Kelly's ex-husband. "What the—"

Vincent shook his head. "Be quiet Connor. I've got the gang moving around the back of the building. When you stopped talking and I heard Penny on the radio, I had them move into position. Froggy and Bear know what they're doing, as they sometimes help me out with angry shearers. Now move back while I do my thing."

Vincent dragged the small pistol from his holster and the cold dread in Connor's blood became even more frigid. He followed the sergeant to the edge of the corner and glanced around, wishing he could help somehow.

"David? That's your name isn't it. Kelly didn't do anything to you, so if you let her go we can deal with this quickly." Each word was interspersed with a step toward the red-faced instigator.

"She left me. Shacked up with some two bit slant-eye." David Windover arched back, his face a mask of bitterness and contempt.

The hair on the back of Connor's neck stood on end, hearing the vitriolic hatred spewing out. This man seriously wasn't fully in control of his faculties. He needed help, but instead had focused on Kelly as the object of everything wrong in his life.

"I'm sure Kelly would be more than willing—"

"I don't care what Kelly wants. She's mine. I bought and paid for her with the wedding and I don't intend losing her. Kelly will come home or die. They're her choices."

The seething mass of snakes roiling in Connor's gut moved faster and wilder. Inhaling deeply, he stepped around the corner. "It's not Kelly you want to get even with, Windover. It's me. Let her go and face me like a man."

David jerked and his knife hovered closer to Kelly's neck. Connor was sure he stop breathing with the fear that ricocheted inside his skull. He needed to draw the man away from Kelly.

A dribble of blood trickled and he gaze zeroed in. Time slowed and he moved. "Come on, Windover. Why hurt a woman when you could take a swing at me. The man who's stolen her from you."

Fear disappeared replaced by a bravado he'd no doubt regret later on. One step forward.

"Stay where you are or I'll cut her." His hand shook and Connor was only dimly aware of the movement behind the man hurting his woman.

"Afraid of me, are you?" The man frowned and flung Kelly aside. In that instant Connor's inner warrior roared. He moved, lurching forward and lunging.

David swung his hand and Connor jerked to the side so the knife only brushed against his shirt. The sound of tearing fabric filling his senses.

Bear and Froggy jumped on David, pulling Connor down in the process. Screaming erupted. Kelly called to him as the two men tugged at Windover, pulling him away, while Victor tore the knife from his hand.

Connor lay where he'd fallen, winded for a moment before Kelly was there hovering over him, patting his skin. "Connor? Oh God, Connor, are you hurt? Show me where." Her voice echoed with terror.

It took another second before the miasma cleared from his brain. "I'm okay Kelly, but he cut you." He struggled to his knees cursing as the left one spasmed. "Jesus."

"He hurt you. Connor, I need to get you to the hospital. Can you walk?"

She babbled and he reached up and cupped her cheek. "I wrenched my knee is all. You're the one he cut. We need you to see the nurse." Wozzel and Penny eased him up.

"Sorry I didn't get the warning to you fast enough, but thankfully it worked out." Wozzel patted Connor on the back once he was fully upright. "Now, I'll get you to Kelly's car so we can take you to the nurse. She'll check Kelly out too, before you demand she be evaluated."

The man and his wife helped them to Kelly's compact blue car, Penny filling the passenger seat while Wozzel hunched over the steering wheel.

Connor sat in the back holding onto Kelly's hand, thankful that now David had been arrested they could draw a line under that part of her life.

~

Kelly looked in the direction of Connor, knee bandaged and elevated. He had only wrenched it and they'd been assured that the injury would heal soon enough. For herself the nurse cleaned and dressed the wound site adding a little antibiotic treatment.

"So, I've arranged for Windover to be transferred back to Brisbane tomorrow. I've got some officers coming out to pick him up in the morning. The prosecutor's office assured me they are going to push for a psych evaluation. Given this is not his first go at Kelly, they have a pretty good case that'll keep him away for a good long time."

In some ways Victor's words were not nearly enough but in others she'd welcome the outcome, because now she and Connor could take a step forward in planning their lives together.

They'd made their statements, Victor had then driven them both home and, after Davina met them at the door crying her distress at the lateness of the hour, settled them in the house.

Now Davina lay snuggled in Connor's lap.

"By the way, Penny told me you'd set the date and venue. Have you considered your wedding cars yet, Kelly? I'm sure my old HQ Monaro GTS might suit. I've used it before for weddings."

Tears burned. "That's so kind. I hadn't even thought of

that, but yes, so long as it's okay with Connor that will work for me."

Victor rose and nodded to them. "No need to see me out. We'll catch up for coffee when you're up to it and we can talk about how we set this up."

He left them, the door closing softly behind the policeman and Kelly sighed. "I was so worried he'd hurt you Connor. All because of me."

"No Kelly. Not because of you, but I'd die for you sweetheart. Whatever it took to make sure you were free."

They sat in the gathering dusk, holding hands, thankful for the opportunity of a shared life stretching out between them.

EPILOGUE

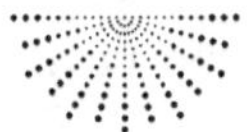

Their wedding day dawned bright and warm, just as Kelly knew it would. Organising the wedding had been rushed but everyone had banded together to make it happen. Even Kev in his terse way had helped out, providing Nina to run the drinks at the wedding. Penny and Wozzel had booked out the hotel for the wedding guests and nagged Lane at the caravan park to do the same.

Victor with his veteran car shining bright waited outside by the kerb, the red and green ribbons adorning its bonnet whipping around in the breeze.

Her mother—Sian—caught a lift with Martin, the best man. Inside the house Stella and Marie moved around, making sure her gown sat perfectly.

"You're a beautiful bride, baby." Ted wiped at the moisture gathering, his eyes gazing with adoration at Kelly.

"Thank you Daddy."

"This time you're marrying a man worthy of you. I couldn't ask for better."

Tears misted her eyes. "Daddy, there is no finer man than Connor except for you. I'm glad I had a chance to meet him."

Simon knocked on the door. "I'm here for the brides-maids and the littlest guest of honour. He lifted the white cane and mesh carrier, adorned with ribbons. Inside lay Davina, who lifted her paw.

Stella and Marie snickered and followed Simon out of the house.

"I've still never before heard of a cat attending a wedding."

Kelly giggled. "Since I've never done anything the easy way, it seems appropriate. Besides she'll go home with Simon and Niamh while we're in Sydney, and she's already used to their home."

Victor cleared his throat. "We should get moving other-wise your groom will think you've run away."

Kelly gave a gurgle of laughter and followed him out the door.

~

The small church was packed to the rafters and Connor pulled again at the collar of his shirt.

His mother beckoned to him and he wandered over, knowing Kelly was probably still a couple of minutes away.

"Watch the door Connor."

As he did a Chinese man and woman entered, looking nervously around as if lost. His mother waved to them and they advanced, then bowed deeply to both of them. "I am grateful you invited us, Niamh. Connor, I'm your uncle Chen and this is my wife, Xiu."

Connor bowed. "I'm overwhelmed with joy that you could join us," he spoke in Mandarin to his unknown uncle. Then he pinned his mother with a, 'we'll talk about this later,' look just as the little girl watching for the bridal car came bounding up the aisle. "She's here!" The excited squeak had everyone craning.

"I'll talk to you later, mum." Then Connor retreated to his place at the front of the church to wait for his bride.

Time passed slowly until he heard the first strains of the march. Unable to help himself he glanced back, his breath catching as the vision of beauty captured his attention, trailing behind her bridesmaids—one in red and one in green.

Kelly's lacy gown of cream accentuated the long lines of her body, draping off her shoulders. The belt at her waist sparkling in the sunlight.

But it was the love he saw in her eyes that captured him, turned his world upside down and in them, was the promise of a lifetime of love. When she reached him, he took her hand and turned ready to make the promises that would make her his wife.

Click on the image and sign up to my newsletter!
Terms & Conditions can be found on my website
www.imogenenix.net

Levia scanned the long line of other hopefuls entering the chamber. The large building in the center of town was cold, and she dragged her wrap around her body, even as she craned her head, looking to the high ceiling. She'd never before had an occasion to enter the testing complex, yet she'd seen the lines of teenagers every time they passed the building.

Once she'd asked her parents why the teens were lined up

and her mother's face had shuttered. Her stepfather had just shaken his head and growled. They'd stopped her questions with a carefully uttered, "You'll know soon enough, Levia." The pain in her mother's eyes had been enough to shush her questions. For endless months afterward, her parents had traveled different routes to the educational facility she attended and Levia lost interest in the puzzle of that building.

Now, as she looked around, remembering that long ago spring day, it was her opportunity to find out. But she felt a surge of concern at what lay ahead. She likely wasn't the only one, given that there were probably two to three hundred seventeen-year-olds gathered in the one place. Ahead of her, she caught sight of a couple of girls, their arms linked together and wide smiles on their faces. Scanning the crowd, she became aware that, by far, a majority of those gathered displayed both fear and trep-idation.

"All female subjects will enter through doors three, six, and seven. All male subjects will enter through gates four, eight, and ten." The speaker above her was loud, and she jumped before checking the numbers etched on the black metal sign over her head.

The massive doors beside her swung open, and now an uncertain silence reigned. Many of the youngsters hung back, clearly discomforted by whatever testing regime lay ahead. This was where they'd been told their futures would be determined.

"Oh gosh, I hope they only have an aptitude and psych eval. I don't think..." Levia turned to see the white face of the girl behind her. The girl had uttered what many must silently be thinking.

Levia dragged an unsteady breath in, her hand resting flat against the plane of her belly as she looked around. No one had entered yet. It was clear many were on the verge of taking the step, but still they hung back.

She straightened her shoulders. "I'm not afraid." It was always wiser to approach things head-on, she believed. When her biological father had died, she'd been one of the few to view his capsule before it was sent into the massive gray structure built to accommodate those who'd moved onto the next life realm.

Her legs shook as she wobbled toward the entrance. Beyond the doorway, she spied sealed cubicles and her heart stuttered. Why cubicles? Usually testing—med and psych— were in eval-units, hidden only by billowing white curtains. She glanced back, noting that others had taken the first step.

"Move along, subjects." Once again, the androgynous voice of the address system blared.

Of course, given it was her seventeenth anniversary of birth, she was technically considered an adult now.

She thought longingly of baby Rald and her half-sister, Elda, waiting at home for her to return, and the celebrations to be held that night. That made her smile. She would need to make them proud of her.

She entered a row and the tall Educational Specialist, the edu-specs as her peers laughingly called them, stopped her. "Present your credentials to the scanner."

She'd done this many times since the tiny implant had been slipped below the dermal layer of her skin at birth. The small unit in her wrist heated as her details were checked.

"Enter the first cubicle, Levia Endrado, and follow the instructions to complete your assessment."

Thus dismissed, Levia moved to the first unit, laid her palm against the scanner, and the door slid open soundlessly.

"Welcome, Levia Endrado. Take your place in the eval-unit." The soft contralto of the voice echoed after the door closed silently behind her.

"What are you evaluating?" Her voice was breathy, and she peered around.

"Your skills—physical and psychological. Your emotional and medical status. Your educational attainment levels."

It was an answer that shed little insight into the many things she was hungry to know. "Why do all seventeen year olds—" "Take a seat, Levia. Then we may begin your testing." If she'd expected an answer, she was sadly mistaken, she considered sourly. She dropped into the seat, the soft leather-like surface molding to her body. "Levia Endrado, you are required to remove all non-specified apparel." She jolted in the chair. "It's cold." "The temperature will be amended. Remove the non-specified apparel." Her misgivings grew as she dragged off the light wrap she'd brought with her, and then threw it to the floor at the side of the unit. "We will begin, Levia Endrado. At any time, should you experience any malfunctions of the unit, simply depress the red button." It glowed and she grimaced. Levia reclined against the chair and waited for the testing to begin. The first examination was based on her understanding of the political system, where she saw herself, and her knowledge of the rights and responsibilities accorded through citizenship of both her planet and the commonwealth.

The second test was mathematical and scientific proficiency. It felt like hours had passed by the time she'd finished, and she lay limp on the seat, exhausted.

"Levia Endrado, you may rise. The sanitary unit will emerge once you trigger the yellow button at the door. Should you require refreshment, press the blue button and a restorative will be made available."

"Can I leave?" "Negative, Levia Endrado. Your needs will be catered for in this capsule." "Why?" Her voice hitched and true fear rose for the first time. Why did they keep her in the alcove? "All will be revealed at the end of the testing cycle."

Levia looked at the now empty screen before hurling a curse word. It was met with silence. The urgent throb of her bladder reminded her that she needed to use the facilities, so, with

a sigh, she rose and clambered from the seat. After attending to the needs of her body, she walked around the unit, peering at the door, but it was obviously programmed remotely. She poked and prodded, but it made no difference. With a huff, she headed back to the chair.

The moment she'd settled in, the viewing screen shone bright. "Welcome back, Levia. The next sequence will evaluate your psychological reflexes, then that will be followed up with the general knowledge portion of the evaluation."

"When can I leave?" It seemed better to ask bluntly, she told herself.

"Once the examination is completed. After the next set of evaluations, you will be subjected to the physical aspect."

"Then I can go home?"

"Levia Endrado, you will now complete the psychological test. This will be undertaken by one of the center's personal evaluators."

She frowned. Personal evaluators? She bit her lip, and the sting reminded her that this wasn't something to joke about. In her seventeen years, she'd only heard of personal evaluators being brought in once before, and that was when one of the girls at her academy had been in a serious accident. Both legs were amputated and her body's ability to keep her alive had been gravely compromised. Her peers had been informed that the girl had requested the assessment before she could request her support systems be disconnected.

"Levia Endrado, are you ready to recommence processing?" The emotionless voice echoed once more and she gulped.

"Yes."

Available from Beachwalk Press
http://www.beachwalkpress.com

Direct Autographed Books
http://bit.ly/BioCybe

INHERITANCE OF THE BLOOD BY IMOGENE NIX

The burning at the back of her neck warned she was being watched. A quick glance didn't clarify it. Instead, she turned around in time to see her mother's face, pale. "Mama?" She took a step forward, but her grandfather snatched her wrist.

The grip was painful, and Kira stilled. "Let your parents talk."

She didn't know what the topic of conversation was, but it couldn't be good.

The dappled sunlight seemed cooler than before.

Her father crooked his forefinger at her grandfather while they stood there. For a moment she wished Vasya had come with them, but he had to work. Just the thought of her new husband warmed Kira.

She only had a few minutes to contemplate her newly defined status as a married woman, when her grandfather pulled at her hand. "Come with me." He tugged and, confused, Kira allowed herself to be towed away.

A glance at her parents' faces stole any feeling of well-being. "Grandfather?"

"Shh, my love. You must go." His grip was implacable and his face stern, but he shivered.

"What are you doing? Where are you taking me, Grandfather?"

They moved rapidly through the village they'd visited to sell their wares just that morning, and for the first time since they'd arrived in the market place she felt fear. What was wrong? Was it something to do with Vasya?

"You are in danger. We must send you away." The words confused her further. Send her away? Danger?

"Where is Vasya?" She stumbled over a stone, but he kept tugging her onwards.

With a quick glance around, he hauled her into a dirty laneway between the buildings. Kira gasped, trying to drag air into her starving lungs. "There's no time. We must get you away."

A nondescript shopfront lay ahead, and he pushed on the door. It rattled and opened with a loud groan. "Andre? Andre, are you here?"

An older man shuffled into the room, bent nearly double from the weight of the load on his back. "Marat? What do you want?"

"My granddaughter. They are coming for her and us. Get her away. Take her now, while you can."

The man's face clouded over. "Are you sure?"

"Grandfather, where is Vasya?" Fright had the blood in her veins pounding.

"Hush, my precious. Andre will see you well." He turned. "Whatever it takes, Andre. Take her now." With surprising speed, her grandfather whirled and was gone.

The man, Andre, eyed her. "Come this way, child. There is no time to be lost."

Eleven years later

The tattoo of her heart and cry of terror woke her, as they usually did. Once again, as she had since that rapid flight from those who sought her, she found herself in a lonely bed. Hundreds of miles away from everything she'd dreamed of, in a house she'd built for them to share. As always, it left her wishing that Vasya had fled with her.

Instead, here she was, exiled without her husband. With a sob, she rolled over and let the tears fall.

Available from Beachwalk Press
books2read.com/IOTB

Direct Autographed Copy

http://bit.ly/2w6g4K6

The Reunion Trilogy in Paperback

<u>Sex Love & Aliens</u>

- Tangled Webs
- False Webs
- Covert Webs

<u>21st Testing Protocol</u>

- Cyborg: Redux (Not Yet Released)
- Children Of A Greater Evil (Not Yet Released)
- When Evil Came To Stay (Not Yet Released)
- Finis: The War To End All Wars (Not Yet Released)

<u>Celtic Cupid Trilogy</u>

- Blame The Wine
- A Stranger's Embrace
- Revenge On Cupid

<u>Single Titles</u>

The Chocolate Affair

A Sapphire for Karina

BioCybe

Hesparia's Tears

Tomorrow's Promise

A Bar In Paris

Inheritance Of The Blood

The Plan

Loving Memories

The Reset (2018)

Hero of Heartbreak Hill

Raspberry Dreams (Not Yet Released)

Non Fiction

Self Publishing: Absolute Beginners Guide (With Suzi Love)

Written as Ciara Cave

25 Curated Ways To Get Rid Of Telemarketers

Book Signings for Absolute Beginners